DELIA

DELLA

The Ballerina & The Billionaire
By Rod Palmer

Black Wren Press
Columbia, SC

BLACK WREN PRESS LLC

LIBRARY OF CONGRESS CATALOGING-IN-PUBLICATION DATA
Names: Palmer, Rod, author.
Title: Della: The Ballerina and the Billionaire/ Rod Palmer
Description: [South Carolina] : Black Wren Press [2023]
ISBN 979-8-9864282-4-6 (print) | ISBN 979-8-9864282-3-9
LC record available at https://lccn.loc.gov/
LC ebook record available at https://lccn.loc.gov/

Printed in the United States of America

This is a work of fiction. All characters, organizations, and events portrayed in this novel are either products of the author's imagination or are used fictitiously.

I believed that if I could keep working on my craft,
and just be the best, then eventually the color of my
skin wouldn't matter. It turned out to be a lot more
complicated.　　~Misty Copeland | *Technique Has No Color*

Chapter 1
Sorry To This Man

Awaiting the queue for her series of pirouettes, Della is poised, in arabesque, under the melancholy lighting of one of the nation's grandest stages. Her eyes fix on her mark with the same energy of that starry-eyed girl in a ballet class for the underprivileged, watching the bullseye her instructor painted on the back wall. *Fixed eyes, fixed head!* Mrs. Geathers had a way of teaching ballet and life in the same breath: in ballet, this is called spotting, a technique employed to execute turns with a magical display of energy braiding down throughout the body. In life, *fixed eyes fixed head* became Della's mantra for safeguarding her focus, by not flirting with temptation.

Awaiting her queue, Della eyes the same balcony column she'd marked since dress rehearsals, but the theatre is no longer empty. There's an orchestra down in the pit, backed by a few thousand spectators.

One spectator, in particular, stands directly in Della's line of sight. And he just so happens to be the most gorgeous thing Della's eyes have ever settled upon. *Fixed eyes, fixed head.* Della summons her will power to, instead, focus on her mark – the column behind the man with the beautiful freeform locks falling around a jawline that's cut like a comic book hero. Fixed eyes fixed head, Della whispers, with a slow exhale. She attempts a do-over, more determined, saying to herself that she will *not* be distracted by the handsome man who suddenly sets his fists on his hips, peeling the flanks of his suit back like a cape, to reveal what appears to be granite abs under the cloak of his dress shirt; he has Della in a chokehold, and he knows it. He smiles, gamely. *He's* performing for *her*. Della can't look away. She's a perfectionist; she must stick to every detail rehearsed, despite it conveying thirst.

Centerstage, Natalia transitions into the jeté that would signal Della's series of pirouettes, but when Natalia's working leg swings out, her toe rakes the floor, robbing her of lift. She's tipping forward. Breathing stops. Violins whine as Natalia comes down hard; her body claps the floor. The symphony falters, uncovering the audience's collective groan. Natalia rolls into a sitting position, her leg bent beside her like a broken wing.

Natalia whimpers as dancers break character and the set is exposed as a lie: not ancient Germany, but the state-of-the-art Lincoln Center Theatre where the white swan, Odette, is actually a fallen ballerina.

Endorphins numb the pain. Still, Natalia cries for the pain of knowing that, at age twenty-nine with her second Achilles rupture in three and a half years, her career is done. Natalia is carried off in a hammock of arms. A distraught Della follows backstage. They're closer than any pair in the dance company; they're roommates, in fact.

On stage, the act resumes. The remaining ballerinas are swans again, prancing around Chandler who dances as if he still has a partner, hoisting and catching no one.

Meanwhile, in the dressing room, huddled over Natalia is Janice, their lone physical therapist, and Meredith, the artistic director who vents her litany of tragedies. "Ambulance is on the way… Ivan needs his toe dressing replaced… Emily has a stinger…"

Janice looks over helplessly. "I can't leave Natalia."

"I know," Meredith sighs, as she periscopes to her target. "Della. You know what I'm about to ask."

Sharply, Della replies, "But Aubrey's got a whole party to pull together."

Meredith sighs. "The gallery is only a block away. You know he'll do anything you ask. Have him meet me by box one, so I can get him through security."

The call is brief. Aubrey doesn't flinch; he drops his armload at Della's request.

Della sticks by Natalia, holding her hand and consoling her until the door bats open; Jare hurries to her side. He's her boyfriend of four months who has secretly alerted everyone that he'll be proposing at the afterparty; this injury changes his plans.

By the close of the third act, Natalia's adrenaline has dissipated; she's writhing in pain, as Janice fits her with a medical boot to hold her leg in place.

The dancers pool into the dressing room. Because of Natalia's career-ending injury, backstage murmurs like a wake.

Natalia scans the room with a scowl. They seem so beset with grief, as if it's lost on them that the coveted role of the white swan and Natalia's position as principal dancer, is suddenly vacant. To Natalia, every eye is puddled with tears that sparkle with ambition.

To spite them all, she calls Della over. Natalia takes the plumed headdress from the floor beside her, and places it in Della's hands. Natalia, straining through the pain, speaks with the anguish of a dying wish, "You know the routine like the back your hand. Make me proud."

The contrast of Della's brown hand, against that white, feathered mantle is what makes Natalia's gesture look, to the other dancers, like an act of treason. Della, as with any time something is bestowed upon her, she gives the same scripted response, "I don't know what to say." Della doesn't show tear nor teeth, mindful not to appear too grateful, so the girls will know that she has always felt deserving of this.

No one so much as looks at Della while they prepare to return to the stage. No one speaks until the start of the next act, as Della waits in the shadow of the entrance, her face illuminated in violet light coming from the stage. Natalia gives a sendoff with the words, "It should've been you... Show them."

DELLA DOES just that, in the fourth and final act, with both power and grace. She brings the Lincoln Center to its feet when Prince Siegfried arrives at the shore and Della, as Odette, dances in an expression of forgiveness. For the overwhelmed crowd, it's more than just the redemption of the injured dancer, or the stage becoming a microcosm of the American Dream (the black ballerina, against all odds, playing the white swan), it's Della's bravura, her dizzying turns and delicate finishes, emotion extending all the way out to her fingertips. It's every pose, every turn, the belief in her eyes, and the weightlessness of her leaps. All night, the spotlight hasn't swiveled so vigorously to keep pace.

By curtain call, when Della breaks the chain of held hands and steps forward, the theatre of social elites roar like a rabid football stadium, both for Della's astounding performance, and for the right she's given them to claim that ballet, as an institution, is colorblind.

It would be sac religious, now, for management to pretend as if she hasn't danced her way into legitimate contention for the now vacant principal dancer position.

Della brings both hands together over her lips then throws her hands open to spread kisses, again and again, over every section. When she opens her kissed palms to the balcony, she locates the man again.

He too blows a kiss.

Ballet and life converge. Her eyes must remain fixed on this very real chance to make history and become only the second black principal ballerina of a major dance company *ever*, the first of non-biracial ethnicity. She'll have twelve weeks of preparation to begin the new season in top form. If she fixes her eyes on anything else, especially a thing as flighty as a man, he becomes the altar upon which her life's dream is sacrificed.

Della has been perpetually single for a reason, though. She can psyche herself out of an attraction at the flip of a switch. Already, she's decided that the way the guy licks his lips is irritating. He looks down at her with the gait of an emperor on high, eyeing one of his choice maidens; the arrogance. *No thank you*, Della says, via telepathy.

If, after the show or later at the gallery, he seeks out the ballerina that couldn't take her eyes off of him, she has a cold shoulder waiting: *sorry to this man*.

Chapter 2
The Two Women

Della enters the afterparty with her ballet bun teased out in a sideswept kinky fro; therefore, this wine-sipping, hors d'oeuvre-nibbling crowd that had migrated over from their theatre seats, fail to recognize her. They notice her beauty, the almond face and bright eyes. They notice her body, as the doorman holds her shawl and she steps out of it to reveal a spaghetti strap rayon dress as red her lipstick, which shows off the sweep of her dancer legs, but still falls low enough to be considered classy. Besides, Della isn't there to socialize; she's there to sell.

Hidden by her asymmetrical hair, is the Bluetooth earpiece she uses to communicate with Aubrey while she works the room. Aubrey, a rare MD of physical therapy, moonlights his medical practice with these events, in hopes to replace his income as an arts dealer. The walls of this glass-front space features paintings symmetrically plotted under the glow of track lighting, like diamonds that Aubrey has mined out of the brownstones of lower Harlem. In the corner near the aluminum staircase is a solo harpist wearing a tunic and gold cuff bracelets.

Della begins working the room, in communication with Aubrey, like spies eyeing a smuggler of top-secret microfiche. *Red bowtie, six o'clock, he's been staring at that painting for nearly five minutes.*

Della hits full stride in the opposite direction, saying, "That's a no-go, Aubrey. That perv, Yule, is over there…" Yule is the French national and philanthropist who donates hundreds of thousands annually to the Manhattan Ballet Studio to secure his wife's, Meredith's, reign as artistic director long after she's been deemed a liability.

Della tells Aubrey, "I got one by the Tears of God drawing." Della eases through the crowd and slides up alongside a couple discussing the hyper-realistic graphite drawing of a boy with water pouring down his face that's so convincing it seems wet to the touch. Della, after eavesdropping momentarily, wanders on and whispers, via Bluetooth, *Don't waste your time with these two.*

Della moseys over to her favorite painting, hoping to draw the attention of a potential buyer. Della fully gives herself over to the seduction of this oil painting of a queenly, dark-skinned woman holding a sceptre adorned with a black fist; her imposing afro is a nest of a thousand black butterflies.

"That's the one I want," says a masculine voice.

Della doesn't turn; her eyes remain fixed on the painting. "There's something about her, isn't it," Della says, knowing her reply would be heard over the air, alerting Aubrey of a potential buyer.

The man huffs. "Sure is."

Della detects a certain slickness in this mystery man's delivery; maybe it's her, the woman *outside* the painting, to which he refers. Della pivots and discovers that it's the gentleman from the balcony. Della, too stunned to speak, gives a feeble wave.

The gentleman licks his lips and says, "I might take 'er home with me tonight."

Della's head turns slightly away, half of a hesitant no. "Excuse me?"

He raises a hand to stall her rebuke. "The woman in the *painting*," he clarifies.

Della stammers – two, three responses wanting out at once. She asks, "Were you, by chance, at the theatre?"

He grins like a fox. "I recognized *you*, even though you look different," he says, with a nod to her hair, which is out of its ballet bun. "*Acting* different too, it seems."

His arrogance triggers Della. "First of all, sir–"

"–Miles. Miles McKinnon." He offers a handshake.

Della evades his hand with raised palms and a backstep that puts her in the path of an oncoming catering tray. "As I was saying, *Miles*–"

"–Watch out!" He snatches Della by the elbows pulling her out of harm's way.

She stumbles flush into him, alarmed, oblivious. Della spots a witness's silent *oooh* for the close call, then notices the traveling catering tray that nearly took her out. Then there's this lovely masculine scent calming her nerves. Miles's body-heated cologne is giving of a warm summer rain in a field of lavender, with notes of spiced rum and suede. He's missing a tie and the top of his shirt is flowered open, offering a preview of the masonry of his chest.

Miles peers down and asks, "You okay?"

Della's head rears back to locate his voice, his face. She's panting and vulnerable; Miles knows it. She's intoxicated by his scent and charmed by the pull of his eyes, which Miles, unfortunately, ruins with his mouth. "Thought we'd have to work our way up to this point…"

The spell breaks. Della backs away, slipping out of his arms. "Work our way up to what…?" She sighs and resets. "Nothing against you, Mr. McKinnon, but back at the theatre… I was doing what we call spotting, I wasn't looking at you."

"You were," Miles insists, quite casually. "But it's cool."

Della burns. The nerve of this man, she thinks.

Aubrey swoops in, polishing his glasses with a pocket hanky. Referring to the woman in the painting, Aubrey says, "Got another gentleman looking to take her home. You might wanna get her before he does."

"Say what?" Miles's hands drops to his sides, his eyes glancing, calculating; he thinks Aubrey's *take her home* refers to Della and not the painting. "Are you two running game? Is that what this is?"

"Precisely," Della sasses. "You think you're so hot, but the only reason you got two words out of me is that I'm out here working." Della is so pleased to take this arrogant man down a peg, she fails to realize what she confirms.

Miles's eyes close and reopen, clearer now. "Bro," he says to Aubrey. "Are you an arts dealer, or a pimp?"

"*Whoa,*" drones Aubrey. Della's face prunes and her head screws, exorcist style, to Miles. She's set to unload, but Aubrey beats her to it. "That was *way* out of line, bro. Why would make you even think something like that?"

Hearing Aubrey's soft-served reprimand, Della's head screws in reverse, back to her friend who *isn't* escorting Miles out of his party after he'd effectively called Della a prostitute. Della's hands draw to her hips like a scolding mother, now watching the boys collaborate, sorting out the mix-up between the woman in the painting versus the woman standing beside them.

As the men bump fists in treaty, Della's hands drops to her sides and she walks away, plain-faced as an android, as if life is a lie.

The atmosphere has changed since she'd turned to study the painting; dancers and the production staff have arrived. Kelsey, a tenured dancer, b-lines for Della, rapping the side of her wineglass with a cocktail fork. "Attention! Everyone?" She takes Della's hand and raises it in triumph. "I present to you, the white swan!" Della, black as can be, gives a smiling curtsy to a round of applause. The harpist runs her fingers along the strings, giving a dreamlike feel. Della inadvertently makes eye contact with Yule; the announcement has helped him locate her. Della quickly moves on and loses herself in the assembly.

Miles, who stands a head above the crowd, spots Della across the room entering a door that's barred off with a red velvet rope. He clears his locks from over an eye and notices Aubrey navigating the crowd in search of Della.

Miles gets a text he'd been expecting. He heads to the exit to meet his assistant out front.

Chapter 3
Mr Luxury

Della's earpiece is turned off. She's stretched out on a bourbon leather couch, her high heels removed. She's just ending a call with Natalia and tucking her cell phone away in the micro purse looped around her wrist. Natalia, despite the injury, is in good spirits. Somewhere between the ambulance ride and lying in the MRI tunnel, Jare popped the question. Natalia will move out of their apartment by the middle of next week.

Della will hate to see her roommate go, but she couldn't be happier for Natalia. Della smiles, thinking at least now she'll be able to get some sleep. For nearly the entire four months, Jare and Natalia have been going at it like rabbits. When Jare spends the night, Della squeezes a pillow between her thighs while lying awake to the drumbeat of Natalia's headboard. Often, a morning encore beats her alarm clock to the punch.

Because of Natalia and Jare, Della has been yearning as of late. It's why, when she was thrust up against Miles, she was so rapt in the carnality of his eyes and wanting to melt into the ridges of his chiseled body. She sinks deep into the leather couch. It's been so long for Della, that her sensory overloads by the mere memory of being body to body with this man named Miles. She churns on the couch to face the backrest where she sniffs; the leather, reminiscent of his cologne.

Committing to six hours of practice a day, Della hasn't had time for guys. Maybe if she'd held onto her virginity, she wouldn't be so distracted with yearning – a yearning that has now suddenly found a target. Della's immediate and full-on attraction to Miles makes her wonder what is it that he has, that's lacking in the Aubreys of the world.

What's puzzling about Aubrey is how he's a personable practitioner and a dogged arts salesman, but when it comes to women, he's a hesitant overthinker. He over-thinked his way into Della's friendzone over a year ago.

The room door opens quietly; party chatter flows in. A lying Della churns on the couch to face the entrance. She pinches her dress down to hide the slip.

Aubrey peaks in. It's not that he's not handsome, with his wavy low fade and the sweet tan face of an R&B singer.

"You doin' alright?" He slides inside and gently shuts the door behind him. He's not so shabby on the fashion either, looking rather Brooks-Brother-esque in his slimming blue vest and burnt tip caramel pointers.

"Just got off the phone with Natalia," Della shares. "She's in good spirits."

"How?"

"Jare popped the question. She said yes."

"Obviously," Aubrey shrugs.

Della, lying the length of the couch, doesn't adjust to make space for Aubrey. She does little things like this just to mess with him. Instead of asking Della to adjust, Aubrey accepts whatever space she's defined for him; he takes a seat on the couch arm.

"Look Della, if I offended you in anyway, I–"

"–You didn't."

"It seemed like you were pissed, the way you just walked off…" Aubrey stops at the sound of Della's gasp. His apology irritates her, obviously, so he changes the subject. "Congratulations, by the way. What you did on stage…" His eyes widen. "Got folks whispering… saying you should be the next principal dancer." He's well aware of the historic implications; it's all Della talks about.

"I'm worried," says Della.

"Don't do it, Della. Worry is a blocker of blessings."

"It's the final show. They've got the entire offseason to come up with reasons not to promote me. Plus the inflammation is back – I've been meaning to tell you."

Aubrey turns. "I didn't see you limping or anything."

"I hardly feel it, but you said tell you know at the first sign, remember? See for yourself." Della curls her legs in, welcoming Aubrey to the couch.

With his fingertips, he prods around Della's left knee. "We've done *how* many stints of ice packs and elevation? You need an MRI to see if your ACL is compromised."

"A five-thousand-dollar MRI, now that I have to shoulder the rent until I can sublet Natalia's space… Great," Della pouts.

"Jare and Nat won't leave you hanging like that."

"Regardless, I'm in a worse position to afford an MRI than before. See? That's why I sent those video auditions to London, Belgium, Italy–"

"–Still not Paris?"

"As I said, Yule lives there half the year. I won't chance even the sight of him."

"Wasn't it you, who said that ballet in Europe is year 'round? That's year 'round pressure on your ligaments."

Della sighs, just thinking how Aubrey comes up with every reason for her to stay, instead of the real reason, where it would at least afford Della the opportunity to let him down easy and clear the air between them, with no more dwelling in shared spaces, with this looming feeling of Aubrey waiting on something to happen. Della replies, "It was also me, who said that in Europe, theatre is state funded; healthcare *and* pension. Natalia and me, we didn't come from money like most dancers; we don't have a financial support system back home. I wanted all my life to become a ballerina, only to get here and realize that I can't afford to be one, because of the cost of health insurance. So, yeah, Europe sounds like the answer. Here in the states, *you're* my healthcare plan. That's not fair to you."

"Speaking of… I got something for that inflammation," Aubrey says, as if ready to take off and retrieve it.

"Don't," says Della. "I'll come to the office – make an appointment like everybody else."

"Don't be silly," says Aubrey. "It's right there in my car." He goes out of the room and closes the door gently behind him.

Those few minutes alone with Aubrey helps Della rethink her attitude about Miles. Aubrey had his hands on the legs of the woman he loves and the hands didn't dare travel to test the boundaries, so Della is never even given the opportunity to reject him. The man's timidness helps Della see Miles's aggression as a luxury.

At a time like this, with Della nightly lying awake to the knock of a headboard, cross-eyed with desire, maybe now a man like Miles is just what the doctor ordered.

Miles let her know that he wanted her from the audience, for God's sakes, and when he found her at the party, he wasted no time actually pursuing what he wanted. Della smiles at the thought of a muzzle to keep him from ruining it with his arrogance.

Della's thoughts are interrupted by the doorknob turning. No way Aubrey's back already, she thinks. The door opens and Miles comes in with a pizza box. He stops and sucks his teeth at the sight of Della. "You *still* in here? Man, lemme get the hell on."

"You *better*," Della says, knowing a man like Miles would go against his own wishes just to defy her.

Miles reverts and steps in, stomping two feet inside like a halting soldier. "Or what?"

Della sucks her teeth. "Boy, close the door."

Miles back-kicks the door shut. *"Boy,"* he cannons with his eyebrows leaping up his forehead. He marches in and stops at the couch, waiting on Della to adjust. "Should I sit on your legs, or what?" The couch is the only place to sit, aside from a minifridge and the floor.

Della rolls her eyes and sits upright.

Miles asks, "Shouldn't you be out there working?"

Sarcastically, Della says, "Actually, I'm not taking any more Johns tonight."

Miles laughs but stops abruptly and cuts his eyes. "You ain't funny." An apology for nearly calling her a prostitute earlier never even enters his mind. He takes a slice from the pizza box and promptly aims it into his mouth. After chewing and swallowing, he says, "Had to get some real food, in me. I don't have that bougie appetite like y'all, satisfied off of hors d'oeuvres."

Della's neck swerves. "Bougie?"

Miles jiggles a hitchhiking thumb at Della, a quick write-off in sign language, since his mouth is full. He finally swallows then adds, "Ya know what they say, the guilty gotta speak."

Della slaps her thigh. "What're you doing here, anyway? You don't strike me as a connoisseur of ballet."

Miles notices how Della seems to speak to the pizza rather than him. He places a slice on a napkin and offers it.

"No thank you," she says.

"Take this girl, you look hungry."

"I said I'm ok."

Miles brings the pizza to her face. "At least try it. Why do you pretend to *not* want something you *do* want?"

Della catches the metaphor: her desire applicable to the pizza or the man. "Whatever," she says, as if she wasn't just laid out on the couch, squirming to thoughts of him.

Miles sees Della crestfallen with this dual interpretation, and realizes he'd said more than intended, but then he stands on the other meaning too. "I said what I said," he smirks. "Hell, I know what I look like to women."

Della points at his mouth. "And *that's* the arrogance that ruins it all."

"Anyway," Miles dismisses. He again raises the pizza to her mouth, and playfully says, "Open up. Say ahhh."

"You make me so sick," Della says with a giggle so girlish and free that it stuns them both. Della takes a bite and the cheese seems to string on for forever.

Miles, pulling the pizza away, accidentally drips a daub of sauce on his crotch. "Damn." He takes a napkin and begins mopping up the stain.

"That's what you get," taunts Della.

"As if you got room to talk. Look at your mouth." A thick string of mozzarella drips from Della's chin.

The door swings open. Aubrey blanches at the sight of Della with white goo stringing from her chin and Miles, hurrying with his zipper, as if caught in the act.

Della, aware of how awful this looks, is in such a rush to wipe her mouth, she slaps herself twice. "Damn cheese," she pouts. Della sees the epiphany run across Aubrey's brow, *oh cheese… not nut…* But still, he's unraveled beyond repair, despite learning that the woman who hasn't given him so much as a kiss on the cheek in a year's time, was *not* the on the receiving end of a facial from a guy she met five minutes ago.

Miles feels the glitch in the atmosphere and turns away, preferring the sight of a wall.

Aubrey looks like he's scanning for a place to go hurl. He's a boy on the Easter stage, the pill bottle in his hand, a speech he couldn't possibly comprehend. "Here's the thing for the, uh…" he stammers. "I guess I'll just…" He walks over, hands Della the pills, and returns with the shame of a perp walk; however, Aubrey slams the door behind him with such force that a breeze swirls across the room.

Miles asks, "What was that?"

Della puts her earpiece back in. "Aubrey? Aubrey." She hears a blip; Aubrey turned his earpiece off. "Shit," says Della. She snatches her purse up from the floor and takes out her cell phone as she paces to the center of the room.

Miles says, "You got feelings for dude?"

"No," Della says, emphatically. "No," she says, softer this time. "The problem is how he feels about me."

Miles gets up and steps over the pizza box, on the way to her. "I ask, because you seem awfully worried about how he feels."

"I do worry because he's really kind."

"Not to you."

Della cuts her eyes. "You don't know anything."

"If his kindness is contingent upon you being available to him, it's not genuine – and if he's not genuine, he's not kind," says Miles. "What'd he give you?"

"He's a physical therapist – a *doctor* of physical therapy – as he's always so adamant to point out. He gave me meds for inflammation."

"Off the books? Risking his credentials?"

Della's head lay back, her eyes closed. "That's why I try not to ask anything of him. He's *too* good of a friend."

Miles grins and points from the hip. "Are you sure? Or is it that he does anything you ask in order to shackle you with obligation. He's banking on you one day feeling so obligated, that you'd be with him romantically, despite what you really want.

Just because he's the one being hurt doesn't mean he isn't toxic. You're being genuine, while all along he's plotting."

"Plotting…" Della turns, her eyes full with wonder. "Everything you're saying, Miles… so wise."

"My mentor said he was gonna teach me everything there is to know about business, so he taught me all there is to know about people. That mentor is my pop."

The door opens. It's Aubrey, looking directly at Miles, as if Della no longer exist. "Just thought I'd let you know, brother, I just sold that painting of the woman."

"So?" Miles shrugs. "The woman in the painting isn't the woman I'm after."

Aubrey pulls the door as he backs out, as if shutting himself inside of a crypt.

Della's head shakes slowly. "That was mean, Miles."

"*He's* mean. This is your night, Della. And he's trying to ruin it because we were eating pizza together? Your night's gonna get better as soon as you and me get out of here."

Della's brow goes uneven at this man telling rather than asking – which, upon second thought, is a hell of a lot better than suffering a man who waits around on her to make the first move, which she's never learned to make.

"We're gonna celebrate you, and what you did on stage out there tonight," says Miles. "I'll bring the car around. You wait here until I text you." He doesn't even require, nor wait on, confirmation.

Della acquiesces. He's taken the initiative to suggest that she leave this place, go with him, told her to wait, taken the phone from her and is now texting himself as a way to exchange numbers; has assumed that after checking his text that she'd come out to meet him and that their night together would be underway, and now Della is realizing what a relief this is, as opposed to being put on the spot at six different intervals under the pressure to grant permission.

Miles leaves on his scouting mission. Della puts on her high heels with a silent prayer that Aubrey doesn't return in Miles's absence. By the time she retouches her makeup and teases her hair in a clamshell mirror, she gets the text.

The moment she comes striding out of the room, Aubrey is on her heels, pleading. "Della, I'm sorry. It's all my fault. I just… I don't know."

Della keeps walking, shouldering her way through the party. "We were only eating pizza."

"I realize that now. Della, can you stop for a second?"

Della doesn't. She doesn't stop until she's at the coatrack to retrieve her shawl and backpack.

Aubrey, still under the impression that Della is leaving the party alone, says, "It's my fault for never telling you how I feel."

She pulls the shawl over her shoulders, "Since when?"

"Since... the day we met."

"And you're just now opening up to me? Excuse me." Aubrey corners her. Della steps around him with a ballerina's agility and grace.

As Della goes through the glass entrance, Aubrey stops inside because he spots Miles outside, profiling beside an exotic sports car that looks more like an alien scout ship, with its doors sliced upward like blades on a pocket knife.

Della walks on, hearing Aubrey through the earpiece. *Only pizza huh?* She turns the earpiece off, and then her cell.

Miles takes Della's hand and helps her lower into the passenger seat. As he rounds the back of the vehicle, enroute to the driver's side, Della's pans the interior, her mouth hung in awe at the gold stitched seams, the touchscreen console, and the hologram of the car's vitals shining on the lower windshield. Della closes her mouth and tries to look normal as Miles gets in the cockpit. The doors lower with the sound of a pressurized hiss. He turns the key, and the engine growls under the bass of the sound system, which plays a song titled *Who*

Knew. It's about strangers meeting on the dance floor and their chemistry is so perfect that it tricks them into believing they're in love, which leads to a one-night stand.

Della, with sly eyes, says, "So this song just happened to be next up on your playlist?"

Miles shifts the gear with a wink and peels off.

Aubrey, stands inside, as stiff as a storefront manikin, while he watches the exhaust spit fire. He's so consumed with anger, he can't see his reflection in the glass, for the reflections in his mind, going as far back as the day Della sat on his paper-lined examination table for the first time, and then their chance meeting weeks later at a coffee shop where she was nice enough to welcome him to the seat across from her.

Aubrey can't get over how Della has always led on that she's too pure to see the motives underlying his kindness. Della, around her girlfriends, is the innocent one who'd take shots in sips, and has virgin ears, always needing lewd jokes explained, which would always leave Della in openmouthed astonishment. It seems awfully suspect now, how a woman this innocent was all too cognizant of how a dirty mind would interpret the drip of mozzarella on her chin. Aubrey can only come to one conclusion: she's been playing him; keeping him close enough to benefit from his kindness, but far enough to keep her options open. Lo and behold, the moment she's pursued by a millionaire-athlete-type in a foreign sports car, she has an attitude. Aubrey wants a year of his life back, or wishes there was a way to waste a year of Della's life in return.

A hand drops on Aubrey's shoulder. His head turns slowly, looking along the arm, from the platinum cufflinks, up the designer suit sleeve to the face, clean shaven and pulled tight from a slew of plastic surgeries. It's Yule, a man with the look of a slick-haired elder vampire who, in his centuries of life experience, sees nothing but futility in the human experience.

Yule asks, "Was that just Della, making off with this Miles character?"

Aubrey's body rotates under his turned head. "You know him?"

Yule wavers a little, palms teetering. "We met only tonight. He interrupts me with some sort of business proposal. The deal was too good to be true. Besides, I know nussing of zis… zis punk." Yule's French accent is so thick, it sounds like he's spitting seeds while talking. "I threw his business card in the waste basket."

"Well done," replies Aubrey. "Yeah, he pretended to be cool with me just to get next to Della. He's a snake."

"A snake? Aw, in that case, I worry for Della, then. Will you call her to make sure she's alright?"

Aubrey replies, "I would, but she's not speaking to me."

"Give me her number. I'll call."

Aubrey's brow goes uneven. "She wouldn't want that."

"If she won't speak to you, who's gonna turn her against Miles?"

Chapter 4
Who Knew

Floating through the city, Della closes her eyes while soaking in the sultry melody. The song ends with the hint of a one-night stand. Covertly, Della says, "Can you put this on repeat?" It becomes the montage of the evening.

> *I wonder if I'm reaching.*
> *But your hand's also stretched to me and*
> *You catch my grasp and reel me in—*
> *—to a space we can believe in*

The car conversation reveals how badly Della had underestimated Miles, although, understandably, the performing arts scene is crawling with men in tailored suits who secretly return home to studio apartments. As for Miles, his father is CEO of Vanguard Energy, which was founded by the grandfather. Miles is the prodigal son that ventured out on his own and started a hip-hop label (which explains his swagger). He's since dissolved the label, but still owns the catalogs of a few notable artists like Skrilla and J. Dobbs. Miles offers up his past with a cool lean behind the wheel, an occasional glance cutting at Della. "I was trying to make my own way in this world, but also keep it fun. Nevertheless, I was busy. Real busy. I became part owner of a formula one racing team, was a minority share-holder of the Brooklyn Nets – still am, actually. Thing is: I didn't want to spend my life overseeing an oil rig or ethanol refinery while waiting on Pop to age out of his CEO seat." Miles wipes a thumb along his bottom lip. "Truth be told, I wanted *more* than just to make my own way in the world, I wanted to rival Pops." Miles blushes at his naivety. "Pops was right though. Real money," he says with a huff. "Real money is underground." Miles goes on to explain that he and his Pop had a falling out when Miles acquired an emerging engineering company who developed a prototype for mechanical trees.

Della looks over. "Mechanical trees?"

"Industrial size… tall as buildings." He raises a finger. "But not as expensive to build. Just one, pulls as much greenhouse gas out of the atmosphere as an entire forest. I had just dumped a bunch of money into the racing team, so I got Pop to spot me a loan… I had lied about why. That's where me and Pop had our falling out. Miles, realizing he's carrying the conversation, looks away and asks. "What about you? What made you go into ballet?"

"Let momma tell it, I was dancing in the womb."

In a soliloquy backed by the romantic melody, Della journeys back to Lumberton, North Carolina where she grew up in a small home on a lot that sits across the field from an apple grove, where her working parents stretched themselves thin to keep her in the best dance schools and on the biggest stages. "Once I made it into Julliard—"

Miles rotates to her with a peaked brow.

"Full ride," Della sings. "So, once I was out of the house – I don't know… Maybe since, for so long, my parents' lives revolved around me… once I was gone, they spun out of orbit with each other, divorced in a few years."

"Man…" Miles looks over at Della who doesn't look back, her eyes glassy.

"I felt so guilty," she says. "Too much had been sacrificed for me."

"That's love." Miles reaches over and takes her hand.

Della looks over, but now it's Miles's turn to look away and bite down, his jaw rippled.

> *I offer you this keepsake*
> *Boy you make me feel safe...*
> *Who knew*
> *Oooo, you're giving me all types of feelings*
> *Who knew*
> *With youuu, I don't need so many reasons*

Soon they're dining in a rooftop garden, overlooking the Hudson, at the elegant Rohan's, in the heart of Tribeca. The city, sparkling across the horizon of an indigo night, looks so surreal that it's apparent that they're out in space on a floating rock while sitting at a table decorated with candles and a single red rose.

Who knew that this night held such adventure, being thrust into the spotlight for the swan role and having her dream of becoming principal dancer now so close – when only this morning that dream was as far-fetched as lassoing the moon.

Who knew she'd meet a man like Miles who, in one fell swoop, freed her from feelings of obligation to Aubrey, and then would have her seated at a white clothed table in the middle of a rooftop garden in the sky, like heaven's waystation.

Miles plucks the rose out of its vase and tilts it to Della.

"Thank you," she says. "For everything."

"No. Thank *you*." Miles stretches a hand across the table and doesn't let out another word until he feels Della's hand in his. "You stole the show, for me, long before you stole the show for everyone else. I ain't even gone lie, it kinda did something to me."

"Aw," Della shies away, humorously.

"I think I know what it is, though," says Miles. "You see, I come from a family that turned against me when I wasn't doing what *they* would have me do. You come from a family that loves you regardless of the cost – and that love, my dear, is all over you."

A breath escapes Della. "I don't even know what to say to that." The air changes, but it's not the sudden wind gust from the Hudson sashaying through the flower garden; it's that Della, up to this moment, had Miles pegged as a rich playboy, but his words wink at a future. Della reckons a wealthy man like Miles will have issues taking a backseat to ballet, or maybe he expects ballet to take a backseat to him.

The wine samples arrive on a tray. Della sips so many samples, she's tipsy by the time she settles on a sweet red. The server verifies, "The Forno Romano Vigneto Monte Lodoletta, is it?"

Della, with eyes stretched as wide as the name is long, nods, "Yup."

Miles adds, "Make it a bottle."

When the server leaves, Della flips through the wine list for the name. She looks up in fright. "That's a thirteen-hundred-dollar bottle."

"And I'll be getting another for the road."

Della slumps in disbelief, a smirk forming. "And to think… an hour ago I couldn't stand you."

As they sip wine and converse, Della notices they're being watched. Seasoned couples gaze nostalgically, as if she and Miles reminds them how they fell in love.

Della, even while charmed by this magical night and fine wine, she successfully keeps her imagination from running wild – but it's definitely bucking in the chute. Miles is much sweeter than she'd imagined. He's possibly relationship material, but… Rich boy…Fast car… The charm… She just might be under the hypnosis of a player.

Miles cuts a piece of Kobe beef away from his fork, stabs a piece of black truffle, smears it around in brown sauce then aims his fork into Della's mouth. She melts with a cheekful of this tender, buttery steak and sweet sauce. She, in turn, flakes off a piece of Chilean sea bass, gathers the mango relish onto the fork and feeds Miles, who struggles to get his mouth over the loaded fork.

Della laughs from her belly. Suddenly she's having this existential moment where she sees herself, in her mind's eye, like a vintage film reel, laughing at Miles's packed mouth while hiking her spaghetti strap up her shoulder. Then something peculiar happens: Della feels her heart open up, this coolness entering her, like walking outside with open pores. *Fixed eyes, fixed head.* She doesn't have time for love. Already, she's coaxing this feeling out, before it fully comes over her, reasoning that she's being overzealous, emotionally, which is nothing but a setup for letdown. Although Della can't un-feel it, she can be aside from it. She blames the wine and removes the moment like a page from a book, folding it small and tucking it away in her bosom, to decide later what to make of it.

"You okay," says Miles.

Della comes out of the trance like the zoom on a camera, back to first person, settled behind her own eyes. "Yeah… Yeah, I'm ok."

Miles takes her hand again and stands with it. Della gets up. He leads her through the garden to bathe in the view. The mesh banister and Victorian lampposts crawl with vines. Below, city lights glitter across the Hudson's surface.

Miles, wearing this sly smirk says, "Why does this all feel like a dream, though?"

Della's hand stops short of covering her mouth. "I was thinking the same thing."

Miles moves in and hugs her waist. He lowers.

Della evades him, wondering what this kiss will solidify. Is it a prelude to a night of passion, or... more? The question that actually comes out of Della's awestruck face is terribly inefficient. "What're we doing?"

"Living in the moment," Miles says.

Della is caught in the trance of one of the most beautiful men imaginable, and behind him, the lighted cables of the George Washington Bridge strings across the cityscape like holiday lights. Against this backdrop, his smooth, dark face descends. Della angles up for his lips.

The stunning scenery adds layers to this kiss; the sanctuary of the garden; the community, in rows of outdoor dining guests, who are as well-dressed as dearly beloveds gathered here for this kissing man and woman. So, there's this feeling of matrimony, for Della, as their lips press and they exhale slowly.

Della's eyes are closed. Her hands roam over Miles's physique, reading it like Braille; her palms supplying the mind with an image without the interruption of clothing. After the kiss, the intimacy continues as they sway in each other's arms, not quite knowing what to make of what just happened, nor what it implies. What they do know, for sure, is how this night will end.

Chapter 5
Lucky For You That's What I Like

Miles's mansion is like a futuristic lair out of a graphic novel, its sloped-faced jutting out of a hillside with a field of solar panels at the back of the hill. Della only has a vague idea where they are. The conversation was so engaging that she only remembers driving across the George Washington bridge and going roughly twenty minutes deep into New Jersey.

As they pull into the garage, which holds a mini-fleet of maybe ten magnificent cars, Miles comments that the home is self-sustaining, retrieving solar power from the panels, water by way of rain and filtration through the hillside that the home is built into. It was built six years after hurricane Sandy; the sloped face makes it capable of withstanding a category five. He says the home is a prototype with over a hundred patent-pending designs and energy saving mechanisms that Miles hopes to bring to market in a few years. He's exploring the other face of the energy industry; mass-market technology to reduce the reliance on the power grid.

Della says, "You really know your business."

"Business? It's my life."

He gets out and comes around to the passenger seat to help Della out of the car. He watches her with greedy anticipation. "This *dress*, baby. You don't even know what you're doing to me, right now."

Della cuts her eyes playfully. "Don't get ahead of yourself, killa." She's slightly irritated that she's moist already and Miles is about to get everything she initially said he would never. She confiscates the wine bottle.

Miles retaliates with a kiss. Della's lips remain shut tight as a clam, denying the kiss, but smiling as if she's making a game of it.

Miles, refusing to be stonewalled, even for play, picks her up by her bottom. Della comes out of the act, clamps her legs around his waist and settles the debt of a kiss. Miles takes her to the entrance. He tries to look around her to open the door, but Della playfully blocks his view. Miles dishes out a little discipline by squeezing her bottom like dough. She lets out a little scream and throws her head back, offering her neck for Miles to nibble. Somehow during all of this, Miles manages to open the door and disarm the alarm with his thumb print on a touchscreen.

As they float on into the living room, Della shimmies her dress straps down her arms. Miles pauses with awe, as if grateful of Della's lil ballerina breasts. He suckles the left. Della's excitement causes the thirteen-hundred-dollar bottle of wine to slip from her grasp. It breaks. They stop. Red wine expands and travels the lines between the tiles like blood. "Sorry," Della says.

"No worries." Miles lets her down. "It's nothing." He goes looking for a mop.

It strikes Della as odd that the broken glass produced no echo in such wide-open space. Della wanders further into the living room. There is no echo of her high heels against the floor, it just ticks with each step, as if sound is sucked into a vacuum. Everything is so pristine, she feels as if she's in a holographic simulation. "This is crazy," she says, while lowering into a chair that looks like a giant white egg turned on its side. She shakes her high heels off of her feet and flexes her toes in relief. She removes her micro purse loop from her wrist and sets it on an end table that seems carved from volcanic rock.

Miles returns with a mop in hand but notices a change in Della. Her straps are back on her shoulders and she averts her eyes as if the mood has left. Miles asks, "You alright?"

Della, looking away, fretting, says, "We just met… and… I've never done anything like this…"

Miles forgets the mess and hurries over. The mop falls like a cut tree and hits the floor with a smack.

He stands before Della, who looks down at her bare feet facing his shoes. Miles rips the shirt from his body; buttons rattle on the floor like dice. He tosses the shirt.

Della's head raises slowly to study him. The man has abs all the way up to his armpits. His muscles are so defined they seem stitched into the smooth dark leather of his body.

Della couldn't possibly speak; even her inner-monologue stutters for the b-b-bulge at the front of his slacks. Della is suddenly feeling the years since her last time, compounded with the headboard soundtracks that has given her months of starvation – now staring at all that meat at the front of Mile's slacks. Abstinence doesn't stand a chance. Miles offers a hand to get her up from the chair. He picks her up like a bride and carries Della up the gleaming white staircase to his bedroom.

The metallic colored drapes hang like liquid platinum. There's a pendant lamp on the ceiling with hairs of light hanging like an enchanted weeping willow.

Miles sets Della down at the foot of the bed and she stands there, not knowing what to do, nor how to begin. Miles hugs her from behind. The press of his body on hers and the sureness in the hands that grip her waist, helps her trust him to lead the way.

Miles's whisper is a quiet storm voiceover. "Tell me you don't want this."

Della's head turns toward the sensation of lukewarm lips on the back of her shoulder, her eyes closed, her mouth a waiting kiss, a gesture as certain as the words, *I want this*. Miles's kiss tickles the corner of her mouth, a slight miss that hits throughout her body in a wave that curves her back and raises her nipples.

"Don't move," Miles whispers. He slips her dress off of her shoulders and lets it fall at her feet. He plots a trail of kisses going along the blades of her back. Della's toes crack from the splashes of heat on her flesh. He kisses trail, until he is on his knees behind her. Della can hardly contain herself.

Miles slips his fingers inside the band of her panties, inches them down just below the tuck of her behind and gives each cheek a gentle love bite. This is really happening, Della thinks. She's in a mansion that escapes her wildest imagination every time she closes her eyes and she's with the type of man that occupies her wildest dreams – and he's really here, kneeling behind her and biting her tush. Della's head rolls in response, her mouth open and panting. He inches her panties further down around her knees. He then stands and hugs her from behind, his hands smoothing up the front of Della's body and cupping her breasts.

Della is so lost in ecstasy she missed when Miles had removed his pants, but suddenly she notices the feel of that hot muscular thing growing against her derriere, seemingly with the strength to push her over – so strong and full of life, it is, that when Della raises on tiptoe, it flexes its way up between her thighs and pats her lips. Goosebumps shower down her body. Feeling his length and girth makes Della wonder what she's gotten herself into, and yet it excites her so.

Miles takes an earlobe between his lips. He reaches down to the panties around her thighs and hikes it up, which traps him against her, bending him like a bow along the length of her flower. Della, like a purring cat, squirms against him, bathing in the warm flesh of the strong body behind her. With the winding of her hips, Della spreads her honey along the shaft between her thighs; she's never been this wet in her life. A trembling moan escapes her, "Oh Miles."

That sweet, sensual call of his name seems to spur Miles into action. Hurriedly, he helps Della step out of her panties and spins her around. He cradles her face and gazes deeply but briefly. He kisses her lips and sucks her tongue, but cancels the kiss too soon, as if there's more urgent business to attend. Della, oblivious as to where this is going, watches Miles, reading him for queues. He eyes her breast; Della offers a tit, which he accepts. His right hand travels slowly up her breast and over her collarbone; Della lifts her chin.

Miles takes a gentle grasp of her throat. Della's pulse quickens. The stress of a hand around her throat heightens her senses. She feels Miles's tastebuds wipe across her areola. He kisses down her ribs and then focuses on her hip. He then trails kisses around to the front and pauses with reverence, his breath warm on her vulva. He's toying with her, ravaging her with suspense. Della's loins throb like a heartbeat.

Miles, down on his knees, takes Della's leg and laps it over his shoulder. Della balances on one foot, looking down, weary with hunger, and yet interested to see where this unchoreographed dance will take them.

Miles brings his hands up under her to support her back. Della laps the other leg over and she's sitting on this shoulders with her crotch in his face. She digs her hands in his dreadlocks like reigns and throws her head back in ecstasy from merely knowing what will happen next. Miles stands with her. Della's ascent feels like levitation. The rippled shoulders upon which she sits, are as hard as granite and trembling under the back of her thighs. She's about to see what that mouth do.

Anticipation mounts. And then nothing. He adjusts under her. There's an issue. Della's eyes open. He can't reach her. Della scoots forward into his waiting mouth. Her head tosses back with a big bang of sensation, setting off galaxies in her body. Miles bellows, *mmm*, as if tasting the flesh of sweet fruit. He licks and pulls ever so gently. Della seizures with sensations that come in waves – a wave for the shock of pleasure, followed by another wave that soothes, passing over her like feathers tickling over her skin. Miles stops, perhaps for a long look. Della groans with a gnashing of impatience. Miles obliges with more soft, circular munching. Della feels as if her clit is swollen to the size of a thumb; she wants to see.

Della, the ballet dancer, is no stranger to being hoisted in the air. She's up high as if on a scaffold. She's slumped over his head, as if braiding it, but really, she's moving his dreads aside just in time to see his stiff tongue enter her, like humming bird to flower.

Della, drunk with pleasure, spasms upright, woozy; her head rolls back and she's surprised by the pendant lamp's spill of glowing hairs just above her face. The weightlessness of being suspended midair, under a waterfall of light, while holding reigns of dreadlocks, and bathing in the pleasure of having her pussy sucked, is the purest ecstasy.

Miles lowers Della gently to the bed and climbs over her with a slight, sexy grin. Della reaches up and massages that thin carpet of facial hair traced laser sharp around his cheeks and mouth – that mouth that had just played her body like a flute.

Miles is gentle with her; his size and her inexperience dictates it. He plays at her entrance. He smooths himself along the folds until she's oozing. Della trembles with desire. Her hands slowly slide up and down his arms, which are flexed tight under his own weight. She heaves under Miles, wanting all of him now, although fully aware of how much of a stunt it would be.

Miles lowers to kiss her lips, which naturally feeds him deeper. Now there's a slow and surgical stroke. Miles gives her more; Della erupts a loud *Oh God!* Miles wants another, so he presses deeper and remains there, pulsing inside of her. She's fully stretched with his girth. She's doused with pleasure and disbelief. Her eyes and mouth flare wide and her hands travel down his muscular back and she gently sinks her fingernails into the mounds of his buttocks, conveying her distress from this new depth.

Miles asks, "You a'ight."

Della gives a side eye and an exhale of relief.

"Been a while?"

Della nods hurriedly.

Miles gazes into her eyes as he retracks ever so slowly which, for Della, feels absolutely divine, for the pleasure of him smoothing back against her walls… he's still going. Della lifts her head off the pillow to look down, to see what this sublime feeling looks like, her lips tug, she's a tulip around him as he backs out of her. Miles stops, nearly fully unsheathed and glistening.

They sigh together.

He enters again while gazing in Della's eyes, watching her, reading her, marveling at her beauty in the nakedness of her face, now that her lipstick gone and her hair is matted against the pillow. Della's sweet brown face shows that she's astounded by pleasure, but the same can be said for the much more experienced Miles. Each time he lowers he's shocked all over again, and the only thing that could make him believe anything could feel this heavenly, is to repeat the movement and feel it again.

Feeling that Della is now ready, Miles adjusts the stance of his hands and brings her legs over his shoulders. From this mount, he looks down into her helpless eyes and says, "You 'bout to fall in love."

He rides with a slick, smooth rhythm. Della, who was never vocal during sex – who would even hold back at times when she wanted to – is surprisingly unhinged, moaning in an airy soprano, now, with Miles – now, with her knees pressed to her shoulders. He slows down again to study Della as he presses deeper to bathe his last inch, to Della's surprise. They sigh in bliss; he meets her with a kiss. Della is fully stocked and piled to her stomach with him. No man has ever been this deep inside of her. His pelvis curls into her with the smack of flesh, this new depth strums a lower chord, which makes Della's soprano moaning switch to baritone, a voice so deep she wonders if it's hers. "Uh… uh… Miles…" It's getting out of hand, she's too tense to breath, from the sensory overload of the spasms of pleasure, the tickle in her belly, the stunning visual of his muscular sweat-oiled body clapping into her, so Della reaches down the tiles of his abs, to slow his tempo for reprieve, to exhale, to process all the sensations, emotions, the intimacy, and to soothe the fear of one overzealous thrust punching into her belly. With this slower place, Della's mind is no longer going bonkers; she can focus on their rhythm; she can appreciate the beauty of him. She can reach for his face and kiss his lips. Miles is suddenly more tender with her. He lowers and sucks her neck. Della gives a long satisfying moan. She asks, "What're you *doing* to me?"

He slow grinds, stirs, each deep caress massages over a hotspot that drives Della crazy. "Right there!" Della moans with growing intensity. "Ooh yes, right there baby!" With every passage, pressure mounts; the tingling intensifies as if she's flooded with glitter. Their kisses burn with passion and heightens her sensitivity even more. She quakes as if ready to explode. Alas, Miles picks up speed, grunting like a beast, their bodies clapping like the hands of an applauding giant. Della is mindless with pleasure. Even at the brink of orgasm she can't fathom how it will play out because this is different. She feels this pooling in her loins and her skin crawls like bubbles in a champagne bottle rushing up the neck. The cork pops. She gushes. She wails.

"Woa," Miles says, in both triumph and delight. He pulls out of her to watch.

Della's body is in a tantrum, her hips bucking and her mouth locked open while she spurts again and again, as if unto forever, but eventually Della feels herself coming down as her entire body hiccups again and again; she's so out of her mind, she wonders if she's even a real person, if she's lost in the folds of in time, oscillating between dimensions.

In time, she manages to sit up but can hardly hold herself steady. She examines the mess she's made of the sheets. She's heard of squirting but never thought she could. "Look at the bed," Della says, referring to the soaked sheets. "All that came out of me?"

Miles spanks her thigh, signaling Della to turn over. She gives him a look that says, *more, really?* Nevertheless, she obeys.

PART II

Chapter 6
The Uninvited Guest

Della's eyes open as if sleep was a long blink. There's this initial shock of displacement because she's lying on her left side, but not facing her cedar nightstand and jade lamp beside the bed, but then she remembers where she is. Last night really did happen. Her legs are sore, particularly at the bend of her hips. Her movement stirs Miles, whose heavy arm tightens around her. Della will never get over the private thrill of a sleeping man pulling her snug to his body. He must've held her all night, Della thinks.

Under the covers, Della massages his shins with her feet. Miles grumbles and comes to. The first thing he does upon waking – which makes Della absolutely melt – is that he plants a kiss at the back of her neck and whispers, "Mornin' babe."

She wants to roll on top of him, take him prisoner and play in the sheets, but Della reminds herself that this is only a one-night stand. She simply turns over to face him, but Miles is already rolling away from her.

He scoots to the edge of the bed and sits there. He looks back to say, "Wanna go out for breakfast?"

"Sure," Della responds with her brow raised and an internal grin, thinking, *One night stand huh… Appears it's still standing…*

Hopefully it'll stand for as long as she can see into the future, is basically Della's feeling. They can make it work. She can focus on making ballet history *and* have a lover. She wonders if the feeling is mutual, so she tries to imagine a way to ask (without asking) if he too wants more.

Miles, sitting on the edge of the bed, looks down at his phone. Della kneels behind him and hugs his neck. She prays that what she'll say doesn't come out sounding thirsty. "This is a bit weird for me… Waking up together, and we're not in a relationship." Relationship is the word she wanted to put out there, see if it spooks him.

Miles looks back over his shoulder, his profile coy with worry. "Hey, um… Della…?"

Della tenses, thinking *here it comes.*

"Looks like we'll have to take a raincheck on breakfast," he says, as if to blame the text message on his screen.

No matter the excuse he gives, it would only fall in line Della's calculations: billionaire, plus the charm, and multiplied by the looks of a book bae, it can only equate to one thing: Della's night to remember was, for him, just another Groundhog Day in a rotation of women. *Figures,* Della thinks, but what she says, is, "Is everything okay?"

"This is gonna sound a bit weird, but moms just tipped me off. Pops is on the way." Miles's head shakes at the text and he even speaks to it, "You petty, pops. You gone fly all the way from Illinois, bro?"

Della was going along, gently rubbing his back in a show of empathy until she realizes that his explanation doesn't add up. "We were never going out to breakfast, were we? Be real."

Miles rises and turns to face Della who is now kneeling upright in the bed, her robe open. "Pops can't know that you're here."

"Pardon me, but we're not teenagers. I was under the impression that I spent the night with a grown ass man. Your father must know that you have women over, and is well aware of what he might find if he pops up unannounced–"

"–Which is precisely why he's doing it," says Miles. "I'll explain later, but for now, I gotta call you an Uber."

Della's hand flattens on her chest. "*Me?* Going away in an *Uber?* No. I came here like a lady and I will leave like a lady." Her temper thumps faster the more she thinks about it. "An Uber, seriously?"

"I blew a deal last night. And if Pop sees you here, he's gonna think I blew it because I was distracted."

Della smiles like an evil joker. "You can *not* do what you did to me last night and send me away in an Uber!" She's breathing hard and burning Miles with her glare. "You pursued me, but yet *I'm* the distraction?"

"No. That's what Pop will think. Seeing you here, in his mind, proves that I lack the focus to take over the company. He'll say that I *should've* been focusing on securing a partnership with Yule–"

"–Yule? Yule!"

"Look, we've spent too much time talking…" An idea freezes him with his brow raised. "You know what? Get dressed. I'll get you the keys to the Beamer." Miles darts out of the room, leaving Della kneeling on the bed with a finger raised in objection, but he's gone. Della sighs and falls back on the bed, still wearing Miles's bathrobe, which now feels like a clown suit.

Miles hurries in a tap dance down the steps, feet as swift as Fred Astaire's. From above, the living room looks like a crime scene that needs to be scrubbed of evidence – evidence meaning any signs of a woman; Della's purse on the table; her high heels by the couch, and there's the puddle of wine, burgundy like blood. Mile grabs the keys to the beamer but hears his father pull into the garage. *Already?* There's not enough time to return upstairs to Della. He could only hope to head his father off in the kitchen and keep him from wandering into the living room.

When Pop enters, he closes the door gently behind him. He examines his son in his robe, holding a carton of eggs in front of a pan on a cold stove, as if he's in the act of cooking breakfast.

"Pop," Miles says, jubilantly. He comes over and they bump fists. Miles pulls out a stool at the island counter. "Have a seat, old timer. Just in time for breakfast."

Miles senior is already suspicious. He is a weathered version of his son, with a slight belly bulge at the front of his track suit. "Where's your housekeeper?" Senior's voice, even, is Miles's but sandier with age.

Miles returns to the stove and looks back. "I gave her this afternoon off. Is that why you're here – because your spy isn't."

"I'm here because I want to look you in the face as you explain to me how you fumbled our future."

"Say what?" Miles's head twitches, his face sours. "Since we're being all dramatic, one *could* say you fumbled our future when you failed to get us into Afghanistan?"

Pop feints a backhand, in jest. "One *could* smack the hell out of you for getting beside yourself."

Miles concedes with palms up. "Easy big fella, easy."

"Afghanistan was different. We were as good as any company in the bid. Still, they viewed us as less-than."

"Same thing with this Yule cat," says Miles. "…took my business card like it was filthy."

"Damn a card, Miles. You don't let him off the hook without some type of commitment – dinner… golf… Try using the Brooklyn Nets box seats for more than impressing women."

"He's French. They don't do basketball."

"Get box seats at a *soccer* game, then. Shit." His hand unfurls at Miles. "And how in the hell are you cooking on a cold stove?"

Miles sucks his teeth and turns to the stove, giving Pops his back to talk to, which is why Miles misses it when Pop gets up from his stool to go pacing in disgust.

When Miles does turn to locate his father, it's too late. Pop is standing in the living room, vexed, as he locates the broken wine bottle, a woman's purse on the table, the high heels by the sofa; all the evidence he needs to pin this failure on Mile's vice: women.

"Just as I thought," says Pop. "What is it going to take, Miles? You already learned first-hand what can happen."

"It was nothing like that, Pop."

"It's like *what* then?" Pop's hands fly out at the scene. "You're supposed to be out there fighting for us, but instead you entertain one of your little hip-hop vixens?"

"I left that scene for good, Pop. This woman ain't no—"

"—The oil field's drying up." This, Miles knows, but what he doesn't know is that Pop's mention of it, is only the setup for even worse news. "We just got a new report. The analysts are now telling me… we'll be below seven barrels a day in four years' time."

"Four years! Naw." Miles swerves away.

Pop says, "I wasn't gonna say until the retreat. If we can't give investors something to be optimistic about, they're gonna start pulling out like now! The stock'll plummet… There'll be layoffs…"

"We'll expand ethanol production."

"The stock's been sliding eight months now. The revenue from increased production will be offset by share devaluation. Can't pray with one hand, Miles." Pop sighs as he surveys the living room again where he is reminded of Miles's error. "You know what… I'm decided. Once we fix this mess, I'm turning the reigns over to Brooke."

"But Pop, Brooke doesn't even want it."

"She'll do it, though, for as long as she has to. Brooke knows the importance of what we're trying to do." Pop's hands drop at his sides. "That's all I gotta say." It's parting words, apparently; Pop heads for the door.

Miles's face swings with the breeze of Pop's passing by.

Pop stops to say, "Oh, by the way, you can sit out this year's family retreat."

"All because I had a lady over?" Miles, desperate for anything to keep Pop from walking out, says, "As I said, Pop, she ain't just some chick. She's the woman I love." Pop doesn't break a stride. Miles ups the ante, "She's the woman I'm giving my last name to."

Pop stops with his hand on the door. "Bullshit."

Miles embellishes the lie. "She was actually working on the inside for me. She's a ballerina."

"A ballerina?" Pop shuffles, in place. "You mean she's not some industry chick? No broom bristles for eyelashes? You're telling me, her butt isn't so big that she has to haul it behind her like the shell on a snail?"

"That was one chick, Pop. My lady is a ballerina. She dances for the same company that Yule chairs."

"You're talking marriage and I've never even heard of her? What's her name?"

"Della."

"What's her last name?"

Miles hasn't a clue, but he's quick on his feet. "From the time I laid eyes on her, Pop, the only last name I could see her with is my own."

"How long have you been seeing each other?"

Miles's eyes flair. "As if that matters. You and mom got hitched in just six months. Am I not my father's son?"

Miles senior backs off of the door and sits in a stool, his head down and his hands in his lap. "Don't compare you and this ballerina to me and your mother. We waited until marriage."

"Della wanted to wait, but…"

"…*But* you pressured her because your palate has been trained by whores." Pop folds his arms. He decides to call Miles's bluff. "You two shouldn't waste any more time, then. Start planning the wedding," Pop says, smiling at the thought of it.

Della has snuck out of the bedroom and down the hallway to the top of the staircase. She peeks around the corner, looking down on Pop giving Miles a heart to heart. Della hears Pop say, *It's time to get serious, Miles. You're about to be a married man.*

Della nearly faints and rolls down the stairs like a log. She covers her mouth to suppress a cuss. Quietly, she runs down the hallway. She doesn't uncover her mouth until she's closed herself in the bedroom and leaned back against the door. "Son of a bitch!" She begins pacing and ranting to herself. "I slept with a man who is 'about to be a married man'? He's *engaged!?*" She paces back and forth, recalling last night, Tribeca, kissing in the middle of a garden in the sky, gazing out over the sparkling Hudson. "No! No!" She keeps looking at the bed, remembering the lovemaking that made her thirst for full-fledged relationship with this man. Della says, through clenched teeth, "You think you can do this to me?! No. I gotta get my lick back." Della hurries to the master bath. She goes to her knees and reaches into the cabinet underneath the sink where she finds a bottle of bleach.

Downstairs, Miles is telling his father, "Let me go check on her right quick."

The old man has bought Miles's story. He looks on proudly and says, "I'm about to have a daughter-in-law."

Mile steps over the puddle of wine. "Really, Pop? According to you, you already got one."

Pop swats the air. "Nah, nah, Miles. I've come to respect Dutch as a man. Besides, he got almost as much muscles as you. Oh, and Miles, you're still on for the family retreat. In fact, bring your fiancé."

Miles gives a coy half grin. "I was thinking I'd kinda ease her into the family, like…"

"It's not up for debate, son. She's my future daughter-in-law." Pop's head drops, as the reality hits him. "*My* boy… A husband."

Chapter 7
The Other Chick Is You

Miles lumbers up the steps as if in no hurry, but once he hits the corner, out of view, he dashes down the hallway. He flings the bedroom door open and is horrified by what he sees: the bleach bottle, Della standing on the bed, her eyes rabid.

She points. "Don't say *shit* to me!"

Miles shuts the door with the flick of a wrist. "Da-fuck you doin'?"

Della crouches as she struggles with the bottle cap. "Last night you looked at me like I was the only woman you ever laid eyes on. And you're about to be married?!" Miles eases forward, explaining, but Della cocks the bottle back as if to bash him. "I heard you and your dad talking!"

"What you heard, was… Look, Della, Pop thinks *you're* my fiancé!"

Della huffs and says, "Do you take me for a fool?"

"Don't believe me? Come on downstairs." Miles raises a number one for his lone condition. "But you've *got* to play along, a'ight?"

"You wanna play, let's go then." Della hops down from the bed and pushes past Miles, her eyes wide with the intent to call his bluff. She stops by the door and asks, "What are you waiting for?"

"You're naked under that robe."

Again Della pushes past Miles, in the other direction. "I'll get my dress from last night. Better yet… gimme a sec to touch up in the mirror." Della slips on her dress, browbeating Miles all the while. She's under the impression that Miles had only asked her to come downstairs in hopes that she'd say no, but she's all for exposing him and gaining the truth, even if it means embarrassing herself. She dips in the master bath but quickly pops out to say. "Let's see you talk your way out of this one."

She's in the bathroom teasing her kinky fro when Miles appears behind her in the mirror. Della says, "Uh, uh, I don't wanna hear it. I'm going down there. And when your dad learns that you were all up in the guts of a woman who is not his future daughter in law, then what?"

"I *want* you to come downstairs. Hell, I *need* you to. But that's not all." Miles's head shakes at how deep of a calamity they're in. "You see, we got this week-long family retreat coming up. And Pop just insisted that you come along. He won't take no for an answer."

Although Della could plainly see Miles behind her in the mirror, she turns to face him. Moments go by before she frowns and says, "What?"

"Dubai. All expenses paid. It'll be fun."

"You really told that man I'm your fiancé?"

"Yes or no," Miles demands.

"Give you a week of my life? I have a routine. I have practice. And what if Belgium calls?"

Miles imagines waffles. "What're you even talking about?" He swipes his question out of the air. "Whatever. I'll make it worth your while."

Della's eyes roll. "How long do we keep this up though? We vacation together, then I vanish?"

"Vanish? What is you *talkin'* about?" Miles comes closer. He places Della's hands on his chest. "I like you," he says. "I mean, *really* like you." He kisses her lips.

Della closes her eyes and exhales.

Miles pulls her hand. "C'mon, let's go."

Della goes, but then snags him back. "You say you'll make it worth my while? I need an MRI. I can't afford it."

"Done."

Della follows him out of the bathroom, but snags him back again. She stands rigid in the courage she musters to say, "And I want my eggs frozen."

He blinks hard. "Eggs frozen? Wait, how old are you?"

"Twenty-three. But I'm a dancer, like… We have a very small window for starting a family."

The more she speaks the less Miles recognizes her. "You trippin' Della."

"Okay you're right. I *am* trippin," says Della. "Scratch that but–"

"–Keep the ring," Miles says. "It'll be worth far more than what you're asking, so…"

Della's poker face melts into a girlish smile. "The ring?"

"Gotta make it look real, right? Not just to Pop but to everyone, your peers, your roommate…"

"Are you kidding me?"

"The family retreat is almost two weeks away. I'm not leaving anything to chance when it comes to Pop."

"Miles, you're sweating. Are you okay?"

"If he asks why you're not wearing a ring, tell him it's being resized. I'll pick you up later today so we can go get one. Oh, and another thing: what kinda car do you drive?"

"Sentra 2016."

"No fiancé of mine. You gone have to park that shit for a while. You'll be driving the Beamer until…"

Della leans in, claps his cheeks and plants a kiss on his lips. Next, she squares her shoulders, shining a stage-worthy smile. "Let's go meet my future father-in-law."

DELLA comes down the steps as poised as a princess, albeit a barefooted one. Pop is hailing her already. "There she is… Miles, you didn't warn me that she was *this* beautiful."

Della hits the bottom of the steps, striding towards Pop but thumbing back. "Miles said I was meeting his father. You, sir, are clearly his brother."

The flattery has Pop grinning like a fox as he leans into Della's hug.

"Miles has told me so much about you, Mr. McKinnon."

That formal address makes Pop lean away and frown. "Call me Mick – better yet, call me Pop."

Della nods in the direction of her shoes by the couch. "If you don't mind."

She sits on the couch and begins putting on her shoes. Nothing comes to mind to speak of, and since Della is horrible at being fake, she awkwardly repeats herself. "Miles has told me *so* much about you, Pop."

"Oh? Like what?" His glare turns this casual question into a quiz.

Miles strains to resist helping Della.

"Well, he told me how you set out to teach him all there is about business, so you taught him all there is to know about people. I've never met a person who could read a room better than Miles." The lie goes over smoothly because it's the truth.

Miles sighs relief.

Pop replies, "Funny you bring up the topic of reading people. Miles gets the feeling that Yule is racist."

Della, with her shoes on, now stands and approaches them. "I wouldn't call Yule racist."

"What would you call him, then," asks Pop.

"A creep. He exploits his wife's proximity to the dancers. He's been known to get handsy with the girls – boys too, on occasion. But racist?" Her lip curls in doubt.

Pop's gaze swings to his son. "You hear that?"

"She's wrong," says Miles. "That's all there is to it."

Della cuts her eye and puts a hand on a sassy hip. "And how many years have *you* known Yule."

Miles counters, "Why else would he turn his nose up at the best deal going? Our pricing is in line with our competitors, plus our catalyst converts the harvested carbon into usable fuel with twice the efficiency."

Della reaches to grasp Miles's chin and say to him. "I just love it when you talk technical, baby."

Pop cancels the discussion. "Enough about business. Let's talk about *us*. We've got a lot of catching up to do."

"Most definitely," Della says, nervously. During the shuffle to locate seats, Della targets Miles with distress glances. He shrugs, as if powerless to help her.

He doesn't know that Della is an awful liar who's even worse on-the-fly. As a little girl, her adlibs would snowball into talking apple trees, pixies, and neon Martians who'd then join her in the giant hole of lies she'd dug for herself. This is why Della, from a young age, quit lying altogether. She could easily pretend; she's an actress via dance, but words? Words get away from her, erecting walls of inconsistencies that will, inevitably, begin closing in all around her.

Pop sits with his legs crossed, holding the ankle. "So, tell me how you and Miles met."

Della smiles and fans herself. "I remember it so well. It was seven o'clock on the dot. He was in his drop top, cruising the streets…"

Pop knows the song. "Oh yeah? That's how it went down for Usher." Pop's eyes thin with suspicion.

Miles plays it off with laughter. "There's that sense of humor. Gotta love it," Miles says, and then secretly cuts his eyes at Della whose laughter sounds terribly fake, as if produced by a doll with a back string.

Pop eyes the pair, thinking they're co-conspirators and maybe he's the mark. Pop, the one not laughing, squints for the aim and fires the question, "When's Miles's birthday?"

Miles and Della's laughter is killed instantly.

Pop presses, "Surely you know. He just had one."

Miles protests, "What're you doing, Pop?"

It's mask off, for Pop. "Let her answer."

Della raises a finger to pause for a parched swallow. With a possible three-hundred and sixty-four wrong answers, she thinks better to avoid the question altogether. "Funny you should mention birthdays. Lemme tell ya a story about birthdays," Della jokes, in side-mouthed club comedian schtick, flaking an imaginary cigar.

Father and son eye each other, suspecting some malfunction, as if Della might short circuit and tilt.

Della opens her mouth to speak, and a ringtone leaps out. She's saved by her phone. "Sorry, I gotta take this." For the first time in Della's life she happily answers an unknown caller, though fully prepared to pretend it's a friend calling in an emergency, requiring her to leave abruptly. The voice on the other end, however, is not unknown, it's familiar – eerily familiar. "Yule?"

At the sound of that name Miles and Pop lean in.

Yule poses a question, to which Della responds, "Miles? Yes, actually. He's right here." She passes the phone.

Miles takes the device as if it's a handgun needing to be stashed. He turns and wanders away for the discussion.

Pop's eyes slant to Della. "He called you? Not Miles?"

"I had a feeling that Miles's pitch didn't go so well, so I had a word with Yule – not that I'm taking credit but…"

Pop reaches over and takes one of Della's hands in both of his. "Thank you. You don't know how important this is. It's good to know you're an asset and not a liability. I see why my son has asked your hand in marriage." A hand that Pop examines suspiciously.

"The ring is being resized; we pick it up today."

Miles returns with a broad smile. "He wants to set up a meeting. He's gonna reach out to his partners and call me back later today. See Pop? I told you I did my thing."

"I should've never doubted you," Pop says to Miles, but winks at Della, who he believes deserves the credit.

Della takes her phone from Miles's hand and says to Pop, "I actually have to get going. My close friend suffered a nasty injury last night."

"Sorry to hear," says Pop.

Della looks around. "Miles? Have you seen my keys?"

Miles dangles a set of keys. Della reaches but Pop parries her attempt. "The Beamer, Miles? Don't embarrass me. She gets the Mercedes."

Miles's head dips. "I got rid of the roadster."

"I'm talking about the G-Wagon," Pop says as he shoves the keys back to Miles.

Della palms her chest. "Me? A G-Wagon?" She's having fun with this. "Oh, I *couldn't.*"

"It's already done," says Pop.

Della follows Miles into the kitchen where he retrieves the keys and hands it over. Della says, "Thank you boo-boo." She kisses Miles and says, "See ya later to pick up the ring mm-kay?"

Miles walks her out to the garage and helps her into a fully customized, matte silver luxury SUV with a hood ornament worth more than Della's Sentra. Della sinks into the plush seat, looking around, taking it all in. Miles closes her in the car without a crack of a smile. "Not a scratch, ya hear."

"Look at you, all upset," Della grins. "Has it finally dawned on you, that this is a terrible idea?"

"It's not that," says Miles. "Do you see how excited Pop is? Imagine how let down he'll be if he finds out."

Chapter 8
Meghan Markle

Over the phone, Miles had insisted on picking Della up at her Brooklyn apartment. He also insisted on being invited in, just to be nosey.

Della opens the door for him and backs in with her arms spread. "Actually there's not much more to it than this." She is still taken aback by the sight of this man, and now knowing how capable a lover he is, she gets the flutters, on sight.

Miles walks in like a model stepping out of a magazine and into her living room. He is perfectly sculpted like fine art, too exquisite for his casual greeting of, *Whassup*. His fitted commando pocket shirt is neatly cuffed at his forearms, where veins like chocolate lightning crawl down into the hand that grazes the interior wall's exposed brick and mortar. "I like it," says Miles. "This place has character."

There are stacks of Natalia's packing boxes. The walls bear square silhouettes of pictures taken down. Della's arms flap at her sides. "You wanted to see it. Here it is." Della goes toward the door. "I *would* give you a tour, but—"

"—Wait," Miles frowns. "What's that sound?"

"Oh you mean that, techno beat… that untz, untz, untz, untz." There's a scream. Della claps facetiously, "Give it up for Natalia on the vocals."

Miles squints. "Ain't her leg all tore up?"

Della laughs and pulls him towards the door.

Miles drives, since the destination for ring shopping is his surprise. He looks over and asks, "Do you have any other errands?"

"Errands," she repeats, with a wide-eyed gaze. "Having sex is one thing but running *errands* together? That at least gives me the right to go through your phone, bro, I'm just sayin'."

"Funny girl," says Miles. "I appreciate you doing this."

Della's hand splays in front of her. "It's not really about the ring, honestly. I get to hang out and travel with a cool, attractive guy. That's incentive enough."

"You say that because you don't know that the ring costs, almost two hundred thousand."

"Two hundred thousand?"

"It's more than Meghan Markle's ring."

"Meghan Markle?"

"You'll make a damn good parrakeet, Della, you should really look into that."

Della cuts her eyes, her smile wide and tight. "So, you already got a ring in mind?"

"I don't got it in mind; I got it."

"If you got the ring, where the hell are we going?"

"To a place where I can do a proper proposal."

Della looks over at Miles as if he's mad. "Give it to me. Let me see it." She's wrecked with curiosity.

"Dang girl. I'm just playing," Miles smirks at his gullible passenger. "When did I have time to get a ring?"

Della sucks her teeth and says, "Don't speak to me."

He reaches over to caress her face. "Beautiful."

Della shuns the other way and gazes out the window, and it hits her, that she's watching the city go by while looking out the passenger window of a car worth 2.5 million (according to Google) while discussing her nearly quarter of a million-dollar diamond ring, and in the coming weeks, she'll be on a private plane enroute to Dubai. Before running into Miles, she would've been content to spend her first week of the off-season binge-watching Netflix.

"I've got a confession," Della says. "I'm a horrible liar. I'm the worst person you could have chosen. When I get stuck, I panic… And let me tell you," Della says, with a warning finger. "I can get real wacky."

Miles taps her knee and adds, "Wacky is an understatement."

Della's lips twist to the side. "Oh, you got jokes."

"No, *you* got jokes – quoting Usher when Pop asked how we met. Then when Pop asked about my birthday, you damn near had a panic attack."

Della laughs and sighs. "If you think that's bad, this one time, my girl asked me to lie for her. So, I was stuck in between wanting to help my friend, but also not wanting lie to her boyfriend because he was a good guy, so… I panicked. I kinda, threw a drink in his face to avoid the question."

Miles shows her a dead face. "You did what?"

"I *know*, Miles. I know." Della's head hangs, amused at her own undying shame. "I'm still sick about that, to this day. But that's the kind of thing that can happen if the lie isn't rehearsed."

"We'd better get to rehearsing then." Miles nods. "For one: my birthday is July twenty-fourth."

"Leo… Explains the sex."

Miles gives a cunning look.

"And you're how hold?"

"Twenty-eight."

"College?"

"Grimbal."

"Oh, Grambling."

"Did I stutter?"

Della mocks, "*Grim*bal? I thought billionaires went to Harvard, Yale… The name Grimbal sounds like a school of Hogwarts."

Miles, licks his lips and says, "Nah, Nah… They're, by no means one of the popular HBCUs, but low-key got one of the best engineering programs in the country. Maybe I'm biased because gramps damn near founded their engineering program and facility back in the eighties. The energy-saving technology I'm bringing to market comes from the brilliant minds that came out of that college. We network with technology and energy companies, mainly black-owned, through an intern program that gives the students premium job placement right out of college. We're manufacturing more than technology; we're manufacturing black privilege. *We're* doing our own gatekeeping."

"Gatekeeping," Della says, as if the term is dirty.

Miles brushes the imaginary dirt off his shoulder. "You ought to know all about it – if the path of a professional ballerina is setup so difficult that a mom and dad of average means gotta sacrifice their marriage just to get their daughter in – and how the white lead dancer had to get injured before they even consider the black dancer who should've been the lead all along?"

Della just looks off, as if she's done.

Miles, however, is just getting started. "We're just following the same playbook of Harvard and Duke, who funnel their students straight to a desk on Wall Street through their intern programs. Someone outside of that funnel system is at a big disadvantage. Can the average black family, in America, afford the tuition of a Stanford or Hartford who funnels *their* students into office seats in Silicon Valley? Know what I learned? We will never convince the world to be fair to us — so we got to do our damnedest to try to even the odds ourselves."

The car goes quiet for a while. Miles looks over to the passenger side and sees Della looking off into space with a vague smile. "What're you thinking," Miles asks.

Della comes to, her smile blossoming still. "Oh, just wondering," she sings.

Miles leans forward, as if a response is the only thing to prevent him from tipping over. "Wondering what?"

"How this changes things. Last night we were just two people kinda swept up in each other. Now it's just a business arrangement, where nothing is real."

Miles pets the air to signal calm. "Let's just enjoy it. Whatever feels real *is* real."

Della sighs, her hands toiling in her lap. "Miles," she says, finally. "We're still gonna be *doing it*, aren't we?"

"No doubt." Miles signals to turn into a parking garage.

Della's eyes cut to him. "Rockefeller Plaza?" It's an expensive district; even a hotdog stand here would give sticker shock. "What you're paying for, is the location."

Miles's head shakes no. "What I'm paying for, is the best. Sheryl Jones Inc, is signature… It's luxury, baby."

Chapter 9
Prometheus

The tiled plaza is combing with tides of pedestrians. Miles and Della stroll more leisurely than most, while they negotiate memorable moments that any real couple might share at a dinner table. Della's offerings are entirely sweet but unrealistic, as if ripped from cheesy romances – like her story of them cooking together; Miles heroically puts out a grease fire. Della kisses him in both gratitude and relief, for the danger averted and that their connection is so strong, it survives the audible stabbing of the smoke alarm and when the sprinkler system triggers, it's like they're kissing in the rain.

Della's so lost in the story, it takes her a while to finally look over and find Miles's eyes steered slam in the corners, holding her in contempt. "Don't do that," Della says.

It's the corniest thing he's ever heard. "We are so fucked," says Miles.

Della hugs his arm and laughs. "No we're not."

Miles suggests, "Why don't we go with things that really happened, say, with your exes, just replace them with me."

"And end up calling his name by mistake?"

They walk on. Miles, in deep thought, finally pulls the trigger on his nagging concern. "You said *his* name; there's only one guy?"

"Our colleges put eight hundred miles between us… We tried, until it started feeling stupid, going broke trying to cover that much distance," Della says. "Anyway, Miles, we gotta decide on how we met. Can't forget that."

Miles says, "We'll think of something. We got time."

Della suddenly trots ahead and rolls her wrist to hurry Miles. "Come on," she says as she goes down the steps to the dry rink in front of the gold statue of Prometheus, who is bronzed in free-fall, struck down from the skies after angering the Gods for stealing fire and giving it to humanity. Della rubs her hands as if it's cold out. "You ought to see it in winter." She points, "The giant Christmas tree would be right over there… This rink would be frozen… lovers ice skating and holding hands. We can say we met here."

Miles's brow goes uneven. "My people can't even see me ice skating. Pop, for one, isn't convinced at all. He had a lot of questions until Yule called your phone. Suddenly, he's giving you the G-Wagon. *Damn* the backstory, as far as Pop is concerned. You're now an asset, in his eyes."

"But why is Yule so important?"

"Yule chairs the Paris Agreement committee on climate change. They're looking to pour money into companies that can help the global effort to reduce emissions."

By the time the answer is done, Della is sighing with boredom, and ready to get onto a matter more important than humanity frying to death from the effects global warming. "Ok, Miles, we gotta focus. Where did we meet? Definitely not no club. I want it to be something romantic." She pinches her chin, her mind working double-time. "How about a café?"

"Too cliché."

He's starting to get on Della's nerves. "Not as cliché as your breath." She breaks out in laughter at her own joke.

Miles cups his hands over his mouth, then chastises himself for even checking. "Shiiid, you trippin'."

Della's nose wrinkles in jest. "You been eating boiled eggs, Miles?"

Miles laughs out loud. He applauds and staggers, drunk in mirth, but suddenly pops out of the gag like a jack in the box, pointing. "I wasn't even gone speak on your kitchen," Miles laughs. "Got more beads than Mardi Gras, girl."

Della clasps her hands behind her neck, her jaw hung wide open, in minstrel levels of disbelief. "No it's not!"

Miles feigns remorse. "I know, baby girl, I'm just messing with you."

Della, massaging her neckline in mach insecurity, pouts, "That's my baby hair."

"I know baby," Miles coddles, but then quite casually adds, "The baby hair of a hedgehog: *Sonic.*"

A playful scuffle ensues, Miles backpedaling from a slap-boxing Della who weaves and thumbs the side of her nose like a seasoned boxer. The horseplay ends with Miles trapping her arms in an embrace that seems to suddenly change from horseplay into something that neither saw coming. Time slows: the stir of pigeons, the leap of water from the spouts behind the statue, the shimmer of flags lined at the base of the Rockefeller building; everything slows down.

This would be their first kiss since the deal. There's no one present that they must perform for, and yet Miles is overcast with seemingly real, authentic, emotion. Della swoons in his arms, gazing into his eyes. Her chin lifts for the kiss – but first, "I'm glad to know that you actually have a sense of humor."

"Girl, who you tellin'," says Miles. "When we first met, I thought you was uptight."

Della tenderly caresses his face and kisses him to soften her indictment. "And I thought you were arrogant."

"Oh, but I am," he smiles.

"Well, at least you've got it under control."

He smiles, "Look at me, getting lost in your eyes again."

"Ditto," Della says while gazing into his.

Miles adds, "I could wake up to this every morning—"

"—With the woman who's scheming your family?"

"But I see how hard it is for you. You're not like…" Miles resets with a sigh. "You're pure, is what I mean."

Della churns in his arms, cancelling the kiss that they were just nosing around. Miles now holds her from behind, peeking over the cloud of her hair, as Della says, "I'm warning you, Miles. Do *not* play with my heart. You say you wanna wake up to me every morning – knowing good and well that when I hear that, I hear relationship – and we both know that's impossible." Miles tries to get a word in, but Della waves a hand and adds, "I chose our fate by coming to bed with you. We went there the first night, Miles. That's an automatic disqualifier for every guy – or are you the exception to the rule?"

Miles licks his lips, "You just got lost in my sauce, babe… Happens to the best of 'em." From behind, Miles can't see Della's eyes roll at his arrogance.

"Maybe the safe thing is, we just keep it professional."

Miles backs off. Della is still turned away, suddenly missing the comfort of his embrace, his warmth at her back. She's down in the center of a dry ice rink, facing an eighteen-foot gold statue of a disgraced Titan God, while hearing Miles's reply, "We can either keep it professional, like you say, *or*… we can just fuck around and find out." Della has no idea that Miles is kneeling behind her in proposal with a ring he'd already purchased.

Della seems determined to ignore Miles and his F-around-and-find-out nonsense, as if love can be leapt into like turning double-Dutch ropes. This is Della's thought, as she notices that passersby are no longer passing by, but stopping and smiling at her, *recognizing* her perhaps? Was last night's performance that impactful? The plaza is beginning to feel like a stage, how everyone watches her. She wonders should she pirouette for them. One gentleman in blue suit and a man-purse jabs a finger to something behind her.

Della half-turns and nearly leaps at the sight of this crazy negro down on one knee with an open jewelry box. Their audience laughs. "*Miles*," Della scolds.

"Will you marry me?"

Della buckles. "Quit playing." She steps forward nonetheless, extending her hand upon which Miles places a ring fit for royalty, a single white fire diamond the size of an almond. Della says, "So, you *did* get the ring already."

Miles whispers through his smile, "You gone disappoint all these people?"

Della then remembers the assignment. "Yes." She looks up and around. "Yes," she shouts, her hands clapping in nervous excitement. Miles stands and lifts her chin with the crook of his finger. They kiss to a resounding applause, startled pigeons scurrying to the air, and tears, to Della's surprise, rolling down her cheeks.

They're still kissing by the time most witnesses have taken their cell phone pics. They stand face to face, Della's hands in Miles's. Della says, "You say if it feels real it is real, right? Just to be sure, that wasn't real."

Miles takes a deep breath. "Of course my heart isn't there yet." He catches Della glancing on the word, yet. "But I will say this: I'm no longer interested in temporary relationships."

Even this response, the possibility therein, renders Della speechless.

Miles half turns, offering the crook of his elbow and they begin walking along the plaza. "Me and Pop been talking a lot lately, since we squashed our beef. Something Pop told me that always stuck with me, he says that a man doesn't unlock his true power until he has family under his roof. From then on, he finds his drive, and he'll forever wager risks differently, when he has more than himself to account for… something to die for…"

"Miles… men have died for women who realized, only after the fact, just how much he loved her. For me, the question is, can you be vulnerable?"

Miles looks down at her through slits. "If you don't mind, I was actually going somewhere with that."

"Sorry. Continue." Della hugs his arm as they walk stride for stride.

"What I'm saying is, as a man, I can never be fulfilled, living for myself alone. For the first time I'm willing… heck, I'm not just willing; I really *want* to meet that version of me. What I'm about to say might sound bad, but honestly, what if you just happen to be here, at this point in my life. What if, while we're getting to know each other, you turn out to be everything I hoped for, anyway? I'm just saying," he shrugs. For moments, all they hear is their tramping feet, distant traffic, and the murmur of passing conversations. Miles comments, "Not the poetic gesture you were looking for?"

"Eye-opening." Della looks away. Sunlight sparkles through her curly bang. "Sounds like you're enamored with the assignment; it's not even about the woman."

"The assignment puts me in service to the woman."

"A woman needs to feel valued intentionally, not by default."

"Then it will be so. It must. There's nothing more important than her happiness as a wife because it feeds her virtue as a mother, for the entire family."

The words *entire family* makes Della coil away, wondering how many babies this man would expect to pop out of her.

"I'm not even thinking that far out, Miles. I just worry that I might seem difficult to a man who is accustomed to women who'll drop their whole lives right where they stand, in order to have the life of luxury that comes with you. Ballet *is* my life of luxury. And I'm already living it – not in the twilight of my career like Natalia. I'm just now ascending. And I'm not about to fold for the sake of money, or even love."

Miles tugs an ear. "Funny how you trying to tell me what I don't want to hear, but end up singing to my heart… killing me softly."

Della blinks hard and fast, as if to clear her eyes. They walk into the shadow of the parking garage, on the way back to the car. Della asks, "Are you always this honest?"

"My bad," Miles huffs. "Honesty, don't win no beauty pageants, but–"

"–I like it, actually. The heck with all the slick talk and kicking game. It used to sound good to me, until I realized it's not even about me; they're musing to the draws."

Miles pulls her in with a side-hug. Della looks up and says, "To know exactly where you stand with a man is actually a turn on." She reaches over and pats his abs.

Miles says, "I just hope they gone by time we get back."

Chapter 10
The Dealbreaker

First thing Della sees upon entering, is Natalia's face angled to a salad wrap like a flute. Her hair, the blistered hue of a blood orange, is pulled to one side. Natalia thinks nothing of Della's arrival, merely pausing for a *hey*, but then she notices a man coming in behind Della. Natalia pops up from the couch, balancing on her good foot, her hands spanking away crumbs. Jare gets up, fingertips smoothing the bang of his round layer cut from over an eye. Dark stubble makes his cleft chin look iron, like his gray eyes.

Della awkwardly smiles and flashes hello with both hands. "Natalia? Jare? Miles. Miles? Natalia, Jare." Della pulls Miles right past Natalia, who turns with a hand raised, as if trying to hail a cab.

Miles just shuffles along, the patsy, following Della who hurries through, pointing toward the hallway. "We're just gonna…"

Jare steps in with a hand out. He's a stickler for handshakes. "Put 'er there, Miles." Jare's half smile cuts so far up one cheek, it makes his eye wince. They shake hands like gentlemen. "Hell of a grip there."

Miles nods. "Nice to meet you, Jare."

Jare holds Miles there, staring, as if straining to think of something to say. Natalia takes the opportunity to hop over on one leg. "Oh. My. Goodness! Would you look at that ring. It is *so* big."

Still Della tries to hurry along. She's been craving Miles so badly that the sex had already begun during the drive there. Della says to Natalia. "We're engaged, so…"

"Engaged!" Natalia's happy smile contradicts the horror in her eyes. She turns to Miles. "We haven't even met–"

"–Doesn't matter hon." Jare overrides, with folded arms and a rocking tiptoe. "I offer you both my heartfelt congratulations." Jare then offers Della a handshake.

Della, feeling frustrated, horny, and descended upon in her own apartment, finally lets the cat out of the bag. "Jare! If you knew what I was *just* doing with this hand, you wouldn't be so pumped up to shake it!"

Jare pockets his hand like stolen merchandise.

Miles gets in a clueless shrug before Della snatches him down the hallway.

Natalia sends goodwill in a cheer, "You go, girl!"

Pint-sized Della slams the door behind them and abruptly jacks Miles up like he owes her lunch money.

Miles's jaw drops as if violated.

Della tries to rip his shirt but can't. "Take it off!"

"Look at you," Miles says, guardedly.

"We'll make it a quicky. I always to try that."

"If honesty gets me this kind of treatment…"

Della stops to say, "Shut up!" She throws herself back on the bed and starts undressing. Miles helps by taking hold of her leggings and walking it back. When the leggings finally snatch over Della's heels, Miles stumbles back into the dresser. Makeup paraphernalia dumps on the floor.

Out front, the sound of the thud turns Natalia and Jare into owls, how their heads swivel with eyes wide. Natalia lay the length of the yellow couch, a leg elevated on the arm. She comments, "Geez, are they fucking or fighting?"

Jare lowers a wrapped painting into a box, as he says, "Swear to God, I heard someone yell shut up."

The couple stare each other down in silence, ready to run interference at the next suspect sound. "Just wait," Natalia reconciles.

Moments go by and then it's the headboard drumming the wall like a beast shaking it's cage. Natalia says, "Is that how *we* sound?"

Jared opens his mouth to speak, but the sound comes from Della who screams as if she's giving birth.

"That's not a normal scream," says Natalia. "He's hurting her."

"No he's *not.*"

"She's a virgin."

"No she's *not.*"

Della lets loose again with an opera note; Natalia points towards the evidence. "Can you knock at the door, maybe? Say something to him?"

Jare pins her with a look. "She'll speak up for herself."

"Not if she only cares about pleasing *him.*"

Jare backs away, his head jittering no. "I'm not shootin' the breeze with a guy who has his dick is out."

"I'll do it then." Natalia motions to get up.

"Hell no," Jare says, and sets down a wrapped mug as if he's had enough. Jare eases into the hallway mumbling complaints. He taps the door with a single knuckle. "Hey, Miles? Slow and steady wins the race, 'k bud?"

Seconds later, Jare comes snooping out of the hallway in impish mirth.

"What happened?" Natalia's smile has laughter waiting in the chamber.

Jare swallows hard in preparation for a series of impersonations. "First, I go: 'slow and steady wins the race.' Then Miles goes: 'Getchyo bitch-ass from that door!'" Jare clenches to suppress his laughter. "But then Della... she goes: *'I'm* on top.'"

Natalia just stands there, favoring her hurt leg with a lean that accentuates her utter confusion. "*What*," Natalia says with the force of a sneeze. And then she says it again.

She and Jare make haste, gathering their things, figuring it best to be gone before Della and Miles come out.

A while after Natalia and Jare are gone, Della and Miles are done. They're waxy with sweat and engaging in the type of small talk that follows lovemaking. His member stands like a pole in Della's fist, his size dwarfing her hand. "Look at this thing," Della says. "This don't make no sense."

Miles says, "And you was riding that mug like a bull."

"Just think," Della says. "A few days from now, we'll be doing this in Dubai."

Miles says, "Oh yeah, about Dubai. There's been a change of plans."

Della lets go. His thing falls over and hits his stomach with the smack of a dropped steak.

"Yeah, Yule says he has to do business in Paris. His lawyers and advisors are there, I guess."

"Yule... Paris?"

"He's got a whole setup. Top of the line shit. Yeah... after you left, he called back after he talked to his partners. Pop mentioned the family retreat, next thing you know, Pop was changing the retreat to Paris, so we can get business underway and — wait a minute." Miles's eyes thin. "Why every time I mention Yule's name you repeat it?"

"Because I can't stand him."

"Whether you can't stand him or not, I think he's about to give you the promotion. Pop had mentioned you coming along

as my fiancé, and Yule said mentioned something about making history."

"Yule thinks I'm coming to Paris?" Della claws her hair.

"What is it, Della? You keep saying you can't stand him, but
is it more than that? Something happened?" Miles waits for an
answer, then out of impatience, takes a guess. "I know you said
he's handsy with the dancers."

Della's head shakes. "He tried me once."

Miles props up on the backs of his elbows. "What do you
mean 'tried you'? What actually happened?"

"I know that, over the years, he must've had his way with
some of the dancers or he would've never been comfortable
enough to do what he did."

"Did. What."

"He stood right next to me, talking about ballet. Suddenly,
out of nowhere, he's telling me how a couple years prior, he'd
been with is first black chick, and has been chasing the high
ever since. That's when I realized that his hand was resting on
my ass."

"Say *what*," Miles blasts.

"That's why, I don't want to be anywhere near him. Plus, he
knows we're not really engaged. He *knows* how the other
dancers joke about me being single and needing to get laid; he
could expose us."

"This man sexually assaulted you and–"

"–And *that's* who you're doing business with. That's the real
Yule."

"How long ago was this?"

"Almost two years. I slapped that damn toupee sideways.
He never tried anything since, but I could feel him trying to get
me to warm up to him lately."

Miles squints and says, "What I'm trying to say is, he sexually assaulted you and you're still there? *He's* still there? You
didn't report it?"

"And be blackballed by every dance company along the east coast? No, okay... You can look at me and judge all you want, but–"

"–How am I judging, when I only asked a question?"

"Have you thought to ask why none of the *other* dancers came forward? I'll tell ya why. Because there're a thousand dancers lined up to get on board with a company like Manhattan Dance. We can be replaced at the drop of a dime and nobody on the outside would even notice." Della is now up, pulling on her leggings. "This is real life Miles. We endure shit that people in your position can pay somebody else to endure for you." Della flops on the end of the bed, turned away from Miles. "Life isn't some playground for me, Miles. And this ring–"

"–Take a minute, Della, before you go saying things *to* me out of frustration that has nothing to do *with* me."

"Whether I say it or not, it is what it is."

"You say ballet is your life of luxury, right? And yet you have to bargain for an MRI? Barter your dignity for it?"

Della gives a warning eye. "Miles–"

"–No, Della. You say honesty turns you on, well, how about this honesty, huh? You pretty much called me a spoiled rich boy and I'm supposed to just take that? You think you can preach to me because your life is hard? You're not qualified to teach me about life. It is *you* who has to unlearn things I fortunately never had to learn."

"Well, I apologize for growing up poor." Della pats her chest. "That's on *me*, right?" She bites her lip to stop its trembling.

"No." Miles looks down and away. "Of course it's not." They're exposed and it scares them. The difference between their life experiences, cracks across the picture of any future they may occupy together; it laughs in the face of the idea that their magical night was the discovery of something rare and precious and lasting.

Miles scoots over and holds Della from behind. She hugs the arms that hug her, and with only this gesture, hearts are mended around a nucleus of silent empathy, the two now wiser of ways in which they must avoid inflicting emotional harm. As binding as this moment may be, Della must stand apart in regards to one item. "I can't go to Paris, I won't be subjected to him," she says, clutching the dignity that Miles so carelessly accused her of espousing for the sake of her career.

"I'll shelter you," Miles vows. "I won't let him within five feet of you, baby. I promise."

Della replies, "Can I trust you? I mean… We just met."

Miles says, "I'll make sure that in the two weeks we have left, that you get to know me as much as humanly possible." Della turns to reply, but Miles gives her a soft shush. Miles kisses her bare shoulder and rubs her back — not a word issued to convince her otherwise, even when a Paris retreat without Della would make Pop revert to his first mind, that the engagement was a ruse, after Miles and Pop just recently started back speaking again. A Paris retreat without Della would deny the rest of the family the opportunity to see Miles as one who is finally settling down, and fit as Pop's successor over the family legacy.

Miles lay Della down on the bed and faces her, kissing her and caressing her face. He makes no attempt to reason with her, since already the cash value of a quarter-million-dollar ring isn't reason enough. Miles has another strategy in mind.

Chapter 11
The Lure of Wealth

Della hits her stride like a model, along Madison Ave, shopping bags in each hand. She slows down and looks over at Miles with a revelation etched in her face. "I know what you're trying to do."

"Exactly what I told you I'm trying to do." He'd suggested that just in case Della changes her mind, they'll shop for a week's wardrobe, that way she'll *be* ready so she won't have to *get* ready, but Miles knows, as well as Della does, that there's something deeper at play.

If it's one thing that having come from money has revealed to Miles: it's that those who *haven't* – though quick to reject money in theory – are incapable of rejecting money in reality. No hypothetical dollar amount can match the feeling of being turned loose with a platinum card on Madison Ave.

Like the luxury car forced upon Della, her wardrobe must also be luxury brands. They're in and out of boutiques that are so high-end, that even window-shopping at such places, for Della, had always been depressing. She's having the time of her life in and out of dressing rooms, modeling the finest of fabrics upon her skin, garments designed with the most finite attention to detail, from a Hanifa skirt with seamless stitching, to shoes whose slight shimmer effect comes from embedded crystal flakes. Della fears that beyond this ordeal, she will forever look into her closet and see only what her usual garments lack.

After just a couple days, Della shows cracks in her resolve. Her initial staunch refusal has evolved into hypothetical questions about Paris, as if only to verify what she'll miss. She says things like, "I bet the shopping in Paris is off the chain… or Does the family have to stay at the chateau the whole time or could they just break away and go off into the city?"

The next day, they attend a charitable event at the Juan Morel Campos Secondary School. The charitable foundation for the Brooklyn Nets' star player, had the schoolyard renovated with fresh greenery, benches, a track, and a new outdoor basketball court, freshly painted with street art in colors that harkens Aztec culture, with its desert yellows and sky blues. Della, assuming her assignment was to say less and look good on Miles's arm, she wears the spoils of the recent shopping spree, a cross-front halter top, wrap skirt, and a pair of frameless Gucci shades nesting in her hair. She didn't know they'd be standing the whole time, so her face is bent with the regret of her six-inch heels when she looks over at Miles and says, "So, what's the week gonna be like in Paris? Is Yule gonna be checking up on the family often, having dinner with you all in the evenings… tea and Gin Rummy at brunch?"

Miles, with his arms folded and his slightly bowlegged stance, tries to be casual when he says, "He might pop in here and there, but he'll be mostly tied up with lawyers and his colleagues from the Compliance Committee, combing through paperwork as thick as a phonebook, with all the financials… patents and trial results for the prototype… technical stuff… legal stuff…"

Della nods away, as if taking mental notes. She appears to have a follow up question waiting, when she notices Kevin Durant, arguably the best basketball player in the world, on the opposite sideline at the ribbon cutting; tall as a pine tree. He looks at Della, then at Miles. He cups a hand to his mouth and says, "I see ya, bwa!"

Miles taps his chest with a fist. "Bredren!"

Della plays clueless, but inside, she's doing pirouettes for the fact that a superstar like K.D. thinks she's a dime.

The topic of Paris doesn't come up again until the following evening; it's Netflix and chill. They're winding down the evening on Mile's couch in their underwear, eating from take-out boxes. For Della, it feels like they're a legit couple; knowing him only six days, though, it's like having amnesia and being told that the wedding ring on her finger means that this man is her husband, because Miles is acting just like a hubby, getting on Della's last nerve for talking throughout the entire movie. It's a city girl rendition of an Arthurian romance where the Guinevere (reincarnated in Fulani braids and an afro puff bun) is lured away from a wealthy CEO (King Arthur) by a fiery activist (Sir Lancelot) who has infiltrated the corporation. Even while the credits roll, Miles complains that the movie is a case in point of how cinema is unfair to rich guys, portraying them as squares, materialistic, exploitative, and tame in bed. Della puts her foot on his crotch and presses it like a gas pedal. "We know that's not the case with you."

Miles, per usual, when he's having devious thoughts, licks his lips and says, "Shiiid... You know I'll be gone tomorrow? Gotta fly out to Illinois for damage control."

Della plays clueless. "So what does that mean?"

"That means we may as well get it in now."

"Look," says Della. "There ain't but so much, of a man like *you*, that a girl like *me*, can take. I'm not about to lose my walls to you, okay hon."

Miles just nods, as if to bow out gracefully, but then he says, "Since we won't see each other tomorrow, give me your playlist; that way, you're still with me, in a way."

Della, from her lying position with her legs across his lap, raises up to Miles's face as if he'd just stepped on a rake. "Gimme yours too," she says, with a gentle hand on his face. "If you really wanna convince me to come within ten feet of Yule, romantic gestures like this will go a lot further, with me, than taking me shopping."

She kisses his mouth intimately, and the rest is history. When Netflix goes idle with the screen prompt, *Are you still watching*, their response is slow macaroni noises and the sound of Della moaning and sipping air.

The next day, Della refuses to admit, to herself, that she misses him. Miles is in Illinois while she's in an empty room practicing in a tutu and leggings while listening to Miles's music, which is a mix of Hip hop, Afro beat, and R&B. Judging by the playlist, he obviously he has a thing for Jasmine Sullivan and Tems. It's only a day without him and yet, while Della dances to Tems's beautifully mournful voice, like the call of ancestors chiming in the wind, Della's heart is laid bare by the first refrain.

> *I will wait for you,*
> *For you*
> *I will wait for you.*
> *I will wait for you.*

It's just a wind gust of emotion, she tells herself. Della may wonder if Miles is having these same ghost pains of loneliness, but she knows, for herself, that she cannot spend the evening alone and suffer this, over a bowl of ramen noodles in an empty apartment.

She grabs her phone and finds the text she'd left on read since last night. It's her BFF, Kamisha, who's just had her last performance of the season and wanted to hang out with the girls. Della replies with two words: I'll drive.

That evening, Kamisha comes out scanning for the Nissan Sentra with tape residue around the passenger side from the year Della had plastic over a busted window. Della toots the horn of her G-Wagon. Kamisha looks her dead in face and still doesn't move for another few beats.

Kamisha gets in with a casual *hey girl* and a leaning hug. Della, fighting a smile with everything she's got, asks, "So, how you been?"

Kamisha pounds the dashboard and blasts, "Heifer, if you don't tell me what the hell is going on!"

Della shows Kamisha the hand she'd been hiding. Kamisha sees the ring and her mouth opens as if she's hocking up a hairball. Della says, "You're not gonna believe this."

During the drive to The Rogers Garden cocktail bar in Brooklyn's Little Caribbean, Della updates Kamisha about her extraordinary week.

Upon their arrival, Kamisha hustles through the outdoor bar's paneled enclosure, and hurries to their friends who are already there, holding a table. She announces, "Drinks on Della, yall." Each person gets a Miss Ting, the signature white rum and grapefruit mixer.

Della takes them through the night she and Miles met, and Pop's surprise visit the next morning, as if she still doesn't believe it herself.

"So all of this is fake," asks Maya.

Della adds, "I asked him if we were supposed to just go our separate ways after the fake engagement, and he was like, 'Naw

I really like you.' We've been spending every day together. He says he wants a wife and family, like asap."

Kamisha's face wears the horror of a Kabuki mask, "And you're telling me, that you're worried about going to Paris because of Yule's old ass? Umma put it straight like this: if what Yule did to you wasn't bad enough to make you leave Manhattan Dance, then it isn't bad enough to keep you from going to Paris."

Maya's head shakes. "You're wrong, Kamisha. Manhattan Dance is a work environment, there's only so much he could do there. If he's got Della on his turf, there's no telling..."

"He ain't doing shit. He don't want to go to jail."

"He doesn't avoid jail by not being a rapist. He avoids jail with hush money for the victims, but that trauma will remain long after the money is spent."

"First of all, that's not about to happen. If they play their cards right, he'll never find Della somewhere off by herself. Second of all, you're worried about Yule's hush money, when you need to be thinking about Miles's billionaire money, baby. You don't *give* a Yule that much power to stand in the way of that." They feel Kamisha's explanation rising to the level of a speech. "And you don't *give* a man of status reasons to think you're not that into him. I'm telling you, Della, follow up Maya if you want to. Give that man a week without you, that's plenty time for him to rethink everything. You say he's a good guy, you say he's honest, you say he wants a wife and family? A *billionaire*...? You don't break up with a man like that, you only divorce him – that way, you'll be set for life. I'm telling you as your friend; take your happy ass on to Paris."

Maya defends, "I wasn't saying she shouldn't do it; I was telling *you* that you shouldn't advise people to be in the company of a predator. That's not a good look."

Maya's boyfriend Tate plays the role of narcissist, leaning back in his chair, casually gaslighting the entire ordeal. "Are you sure he don't got five different chicks in five different cities, with each of them thinking *they're* the one? They control women by making them think they got a real grab for the bag. That's how rich brothas do."

On behalf of everyone, Maya gives Tate an open hand to talk to. She then asks, "So, how's Aubrey taking it?"

Tate groans in pained empathy for the man.

"I'll *show* you how Aubrey's taking it." Della sets her phone on the table, showing a thread of texts calling her gullible, a broke bitch, and gold-digger among other things.

"And you're not gonna clap back?" Kamisha snatches the phone to do the honors.

Della takes the phone back. "Even better, I'm gonna let him keep going. Let him provide justification for a restraining order." Della's fingernail taps her phone screen. "*This* is the real Aubrey. I want nothing to do with him."

"Question," says Tate, as if his concern had been marinating for a while now. "Probably took buddy a while to amass all that wealth, right? So, how old is he? How does he look?"

Kamisha's eyes fall closed. "Child, I was afraid to ask."

"Weeell," Della says. "He texted me that he's back in town, and I sent him the location, so you're about to see him in a minute."

In the meantime, they find other things to talk about, like New York governor Cuomo's sexual harassment scandal; Brooklyn's string of shootings the day before, leaving ten people wounded, which is all over the news.

They're discussing their forecasts for the fifth season of Insecure, when the bright colored artwork along the paneled enclosure opens up.

In walks a talk dark man in a relaxed knit shirt settled into his defined body. Della's back is turned. Kamisha is the first to see him, with dreadlocks falling softly around his chiseled face, which turns like a boat's prow, searching for someone in particular.

Kamisha raises holy hands. "Don't tell me that's him!"

Della looks back then rises to her feet.

"Dammit, Maya, that's him!" Kamisha falls prostrate across the table, grabbing Maya's hand for strength.

Maya snatches out of the vicelike grip, miming pain, examining a hand now mangled like a chicken foot.

Back at Miles's place, Della is ready to inform him that she'll go to Paris. She's standing in his closet, finding her clothing clean, pressed, and hanging, courtesy of the maid. Missing Miles while he was gone has helped Della realize the presence of a bond, and out of that bond, trust — if only by way of familiarity. She now feels like she can trust him enough to protect her over a span of days at a resort where the man who once assaulted her would be lurking the hallways like a shark. With such risk weighed upon this trust, understandably, Della hits the roof the moment that trust is violated.

She's in the closet listening to her own heart, when there's an interference. She hears the voice of Miles talking on the phone, but then a woman's voice replies. She sounds too casual for it to be a business call. Della quiets her thoughts and tunes her ears to the conversation around the corner. "Don't give me that look," the woman says.

Della thinks, *They must be facetiming.*

The woman adds, "You're the one who flew out and didn't even come see me."

Della remembers Tate saying how rich men have chicks plotted in multiple cities. *Am I the Brooklyn chick?*

"I was busy," says Miles. "Just like I'm busy now."

Hurrying her off the phone before you get caught?

"Busy doing what — with your shirt off."

Mighty comfortable facetime-ing with no shirt. She's seen his body before, obviously.

"None of your business," Miles says.

"Whatever. Love you."

Miles replies, "Love you too, big head."

Della is so upset, she's ready to combust. She cracks her knuckles and walks in just as the call ends. "Didn't know I was standing right there in the closet, did you?"

Miles lay back on the bed, hands clasped behind his head and his feet crossed. "Girl what you talking about?"

Della marches over and slaps his feet uncrossed. "I heard you! You and your little bitch! I heard everything!" Della boils at the fact that Miles is smiling.

Casually, he says, "I don't take too kindly to you calling my little sister a bitch."

In just a flutter of eye blinks, the evidence comes together: of course, he's comfortable enough to facetime his sister without a shirt; the *I love you bighead*, sounds like a comment a big brother would make; Vanguard Energy's headquarters, where Miles flew out to, is also where his family lives, so his sister was on his case about visiting the city and not her.

Della flops on the bed with a deep sigh of both relief and regret. "I was so ready to believe… You see, Tate was saying how rich guys have multiple women in multiple cities and… My bad, Miles."

"You're the only one Della. I was celibate for months before I met you, so there isn't even a maybe out there."

"Sorry I hit you."

"And if this Tate dude really knew how rich men operate, he'd be one."

Della crawls on the bed, lays her head on Miles's chest and says, "I was just about to say yes, that I'll go with you to Paris." She raises a finger, "But you've gotta protect me from Yule."

Miles squeezes her. "Promise, I won't let him near you."

ON THE DAY of departure, it feels like a dream, being on Miles's arm, sashaying across the tarmac in a gold Hanifa layered tassel skirt, a limited edition Vellies bag, and a gold pointed-toe mule. This dream, however, is not tempered by the realities of adulthood. Looking over at Mile's sun-splashed face awakens her girlish dreams of a Prince Charming, before society told her to reject chivalry and decadence. Dating, as an adult, has trained Della's emotional palate toward more realistic fancies, like quiet afternoons and sentimental gestures. Expect too much from a man – who is really just another adult skimming by every month – and he'll flee from the pressure. For Miles, there *is* no such pressure. In Miles's world, the things of Della's wildest dreams are already a solid reality.

For Miles, on the other hand, pressure isn't just Della's petite dancer body, her gorgeous head of natural hair, nor her thick Nubian lips glistening in this golden morning sun. Pressure is a woman whose principal source of contentment comes from herself. For Della, it will always be ballet, so even with a billionaire like Miles, she has the freedom to be herself – not tiptoeing around him, or folding like the women who are so desperate to secure the relationship, that they try to be who they think Miles wants them to be. Little does Della know, the moment that she made the joke about Miles's breath at the Rockefeller plaza, his immediate thought was, *Oh yeah, that's wifey there.* Pressure, for Miles, is authenticity.

It certainly doesn't hurt, though, if the way she glows in the sun makes him think fondly of a future sunrise, with her, overlooking a Nairobi horizon.

They scale the steps to the jet, the sun orange on their backs and on the broadside of the iron vessel. The copilot helps Della up by the hand that wears an engagement ring so magnificently cut, it produces a sun flare.

The jet's interior is plush. Della didn't expect wood grain and tan leather, nor the big screen and couch.

She and Miles are the first in the family to arrive. Della sits upright. She doesn't lounge in the couch; she's suddenly nervous in this plush belly of the plane. They've had a week to rehearse the details of their imaginary relationship to perfection, yet now with the moment upon her, Della is haunted by daymares of having a meltdown in front of Miles's family.

PART III

Chapter 12
Just A Ballerina

Sage, Miles's mother, favors Susan Taylor the long-time editor of Essence Magazine. She boards the plane and comes right to Della. As they squeeze hands an air kiss, Della cuts an eye and says, "Has anyone told you that you look just like–"

"–Angela Bassett? Girl, I get that all the time."

Della pauses, stupidly. Miles shuffles away to hide his grin. Della recovers with a clean smile and says, "I *see* where Miles gets his looks."

Pop protests, frowning with an index finger to his chest. "But I thought you said–"

"–That you look young, Pop. *Young.*" Meaning not handsome, but Della's delivery, how her head-turn dials to him, displaying an expression of playful condescendence, is memeworthy. It gives them a good laugh to start the ten-hour flight.

Boarding just in time for Della's punchline is the youngest, Madison. "I like her already." She's model thin with cat eyes and shoulder length hair. Complexion aside, Madison looks quite different, as if all the clan's recessive traits surfaced in her.

Sage's "first born" and Vanguard Energy's Chief of Operations, carries a portfolio of some sort. She also carries her mother's facial features, with this oddly beautiful and benevolent gait. Brooke forces a smile and gives an uninspired, "I'm here."

"She'll be alright," Sage says, wearily.

Eliza, in charge of Public Relations for Vanguard energy, exudes mystic energy, with a necklace of stones, bundled dreadlocks with two blades down each side of her face and white highlights at the corners of her eyes. Her presence is giving Black Panther high-profile extra, holding a suspect gaze while delivering her only line, "So *this* is the mystery woman."

Eliza then steps aside to present her other half. "This is Joelle, my spouse–"

"–Husband," Joelle corrects. "They call me Dutch."

"Nice to meet you Dutch," Della says, as unaffectedly as she can, while suffering the pressure from Dutch's tight handshake along with the pressure to not stare at Dutch's absent breasts. Della makes a mental note to be mindful of Dutch's pronouns.

There's an older gentleman boarding last. Della motions toward him for an introduction, but Miles holds her back and whispers, "That's Sims, our security."

The pilot comes in over the intercom; the chatter ceases, and they buckle up for takeoff. By the time the plane rumbles down the runway and noses up, Miles is asleep. His head tilts back with his mouth open. Della tries squeezing his hand and poking his ribs, only to learn that he's a hard sleeper. Della feels insecure, now, having to go it alone so soon with Miles's folks. The plane levels off and Miles's head lops over on Della's shoulder; she curses him under her breath.

Pop, sitting across the aisle, is up for small talk. He looks over at Della and says, "Actually we're missing one, Corine, our second oldest. Busy schedule. She's an international lawyer assisting Caribbean nations to hopefully succeed the British Monarch in a few years."

A wide-eyed Della parrots, "Succeed the British Monarch? What on earth are you talking about, Pop?" This is unfathomable, to her.

"Yes," nods Pop. "Here it is, 2021 and imperialism is still a reality. British Parliament appoints Caribbean Prime Ministers and controls their foreign trade deals."

Della squints and her head shakes.

Pop adds, "I love all my children the same, but I'm most proud of Corine. I told all my children they have three options: work for the family business, go into politics, or go change the world. Corine: she decided to change the world." Pop cuts an eye at Madison over on the couch, primping her hair for a selfie; she's the one who seems disinterested in either of the three options.

Della leans toward the aisle, inquiring, "Pop. You say politics *or* change the world? They don't go hand in hand?"

Pop chuckles. "I must've forgotten who I was talking to." He adjusts in his chair. "Young lady… If a child of mine gets into politics, it would be just another way for them to work for the family business, ya know?" Pop then points over at Miles and says, "You might wanna straighten him up before he gets a stiff neck. Sage and I… we'll be in the back if you need anything." Pop helps Sage up from her seat and the two disappear for most of the flight.

Aside from meal time, there's no point at which everyone is awake at once, so Della would find herself up with various family members, silence forcing conversation, where Della learns a few things about Miles's family.

Eliza and Dutch have been married two years. Their playful argument over the movie selection, has Della smiling fondly upon them. When Eliza excuses herself to the restroom, is where the tea begins. Dutch glances around and asks, "Know why they call me Dutch?"

Della dare not say, but thinks of the term *going Dutch*, where that dinner tab is perhaps metaphoric of his gender: split between male and female.

Dutch says, "I'll give you a hint: Dutch Masters."

The hint doesn't help Della because the only thing she's ever smoked in life was southern barbecue with her father.

Dutch sighs, "I got the name in my college. Couldn't nobody roll a blunt like me. I was thugged out, back then."

Della figures it wise to pose a question indicative of one marrying into the McKinnon family. "So, Dutch… You've had some time to get to know this family. Is there anything you wanna tell me?"

"I don't know." Dutch rubs his chin, pondering. "The thing is, *my* entrance into this family won't bear any resemblance to yours."

Delicately, Della says, "They certainly seem accepting of you now. They weren't in the beginning?"

"At all," Dutch replies, but then redirects with a pointed finger. "But *you'll* have a harder time than even someone like me. You see, I come from money. I provide for my woman – but you? You're gonna be provided *for.*" Dutch smooths his crown of waves. "You signed a prenup yet?"

Della's head shakes. "Haven't thought that far ahead."

Dutch frowns, "No? Not with that big ole ring sittin' on your fanger?" Dutch glances for secrecy. "I advise you to talk to a lawyer; this family's prenup is a *problem* – not for me though. Eliza might've have slid me a prenup, but at the same time, I had one waiting in the cut for her."

"If you don't mind me asking, Dutch, where does your money come from?"

All before Eliza returns, Dutch has time to explain his role in the family empire. His surname, Stroud, harkens respect in the trucking industry. "Girl, I can drive eighteen wheelers and everythang," Dutch says, with a hand shifting imaginary gears.

"I'm mad nice wit it, too." And to enlighten Della on the echelon in which he occupies, Dutch explains how his family and a few joint investors recently "put a million" on a politician.

"Wait, what?" Della frowns. "You say it like it's a hit."

It's campaign contributions for the gubernatorial race in Nebraska. It's their attempt to unseat the incumbent, for a candidate who promises not only to back their proposal for a central distribution center, but also vows to load the deal with corporate incentives for the jobs they'll bring to the state and to the economically depressed county of Dundy, Nebraska where the site would be located.

Eliza returns from the restroom and Dutch gets up to take his turn. Della, watching Dutch walk away, is astounded at what she sees. The one dead giveaway that Dutch was being born female, is his yams. The upper body is masculine, but the yams have twice the bulk of his wife's.

Eliza sits, aims the remote and is content to scroll through the movie selection screen without a mumbling word. Perhaps the chakra stones around Eliza's neck picks up an energy of deception, with which she refuses to comingle, even for the sake of being cordial.

Della dozes off for what feels like five minutes, but upon waking, the big screen rolls the closing credits of a whole movie, and it's now Madison on the couch with her. Madison and Miles are in the middle of playing the dozens, like any older brother would tease his baby sister, only Madison and Della are the same age, which makes Della wonder how Miles really sees her.

Madison and Della's conversation is all about fashion. She promises to take Della shopping at Rue De Rivoli and St. Paul Village. Madison, who hasn't taken to either of Pop's 'three options,' makes her own money as an Instagram fashionista and blogger. Madison has so many followers that she can charge major brands, per ad, up to half of Della's annual take-home.

Della rides out the remainder of her flight by a window seat, watching the clouds below and dozing in and out of sleep, thinking how everyone on the flight seems to be doing something noteworthy, while Della practices thirty hours a week year-round, just to dance to an audience of snobs, for hardly a living wage. Even Sims, the security, at one point has a brief conversation with Della where he mentions that he had a long career with Secret Service, where he delayed starting his own security firm just so he could serve the Obamas.

Della looks down at her designer dress and shoes and it feels like a costume. Never, in all of her years, has Della's mind produced the thought that she's *just* a ballet dancer.

Chapter 13
Exposed

A stretch limo with flags on the hood, shuttles them from the airstrip like an ambassador's escort.

After a half hour drive, they pass through an iron gate with security, and a view of the estate opens around the bend. Bright green grass stretches as far and wide as the eye can see. To Della, the word chateau always meant a small and quaint abode, but this large structure coming into view around the final bend of the long winding road, is but a drawbridge and moat short of a castle. There's a golf course and a garden bursting with colorful flowers and exotic trees. There's a number of ponds large and small. There's also an industrial windmill in the back, and a vineyard with vines tamed around rows of mesh, loaded with bunches of purple grapes. There's another large facility with a fleet of wine trucks bearing the same trident logo at the center of the iron gate.

YULE is out front to greet them. Della's skin crawls at the sight of him. Yule patiently greets and compliments everyone, saving Della for last. Della pumps Miles's hand, letting him know that she'll allow it.

Yule takes her handshake and folds it into a hug. He's a wily veteran at turning an inch into a mile before you know it. Yule urges the others to go ahead and follow the concierge. "Della and I will catch up."

Miles slides over and pulls Della out of Yule's personal space and into his. "No disrespect, but Della and me, we're a package deal."

Yule eyes Della. "Congratulations on your engagement, madame… monsieur. I fear I might lose another dancer to marriage," he says, with a hock on the double r in marriage.

Della smiles, content with a nonreply.

Yule hurries to the front as they enter the chateau. The place is so immense, Della feels as if she's walking into the face of a mountain.

Yule takes over the role of tour guide for his honored guests. The foyer displays as many artifacts as a museum. The front desk of well-groomed staff, dressed in muted colors, has the feel of a pricey resort.

They go, in file, down a hallway with pictures of Yule shaking hands with prime ministers, sultans, and American tech giants. One picture that stands out to Miles; he whispers, "Haliburton" —as if the name should mean something to Della. They enter an awe-inspiring ballroom with a centerpiece chandelier that seems to weigh a ton.

Yule does an abbreviated tour, giving a rundown of his family tree, the branches of nobility that the care of this chateau has passed through. They walk past a dark staircase tied off with rope that Yule seems content to leave it up to the imagination.

Sage says, "We're just going to waltz past this? What's down there?"

Yule seems caught off guard; he gulps before answering, "It's… the dungeons – gently used. It actually served as a safe haven for Jewish people during German occupation."

Miles whispers from the side of his mouth, "And a hundred years before that?"

"Slave quarters," Della adds.

Soon they arrive at the wing that's reserved for the McKinnons. Yule is near the end of his presentation, where he details the last of his many renovations to turn this once condemned "chateau" into the grand resort that it is today, now available to the public; the one percent of the public that can afford it.

Della and Miles's room is the last stop. Yule opens the door with a magnetic card and hands a pair of card keys to Miles and Della, while bigging them adieu.

Della and Miles enter and close the door behind them, but Yule stops the door-swing with a foot. "Della?" He makes praying hands. "A moment of your time please."

Miles seems ready to run interference, but Della's expression says she'll allow Yule's request, guessing they might discuss her promotion.

Della and Yule stand just outside the room's closed door, in a hallway as large as subway tunnel, with stone tiled floors and clerestory, stained glass windows, which Yule previously said was salvaged from the Palace of Versailles before it was demolished.

"Impressive ring," says Yule.

"I thought this was about ballet."

"Oh, but it is, madame," Yule laughs. His laugh lines cut like the seams of a puppet, a diabolical, horror puppet.

Della suppresses her disgust.

"We will be convening soon concerning your possible promotion. If talent were the only issue, why, there would be nothing to discuss."

"If not talent, what else?" Della almost wonders if — for the first time in her ballet career — she'll get a candid admission that race *is* a factor.

"Commitment," Yule says. "That ring changes your commitment – as if you were not already sending auditions tapes around Europe."

"Wait." Della sighs. "How do you know about that?"

He learned from Aubrey, but the lie he tells is, "We were contacted about a reference."

Della resists the urge to ask from whom, or from which country. "My overseas interest was influenced by finances. I'm underpaid. A principal dancer salary will solve that."

Yule folds his arms and rubs his chin in confusion. "The principal dancer's salary solves it, you say?"

Della looks him over. "You heard right."

"I heard you the first time. I repeated it so you could hear *yourself*." Yule is overcome with distress, as if trapped within his own shrugging shoulders, powerless to come to any other conclusion but this: "The fact that it didn't dawn on you that you're marrying into a situation that already 'solves' the financial issue, proves that this engagement – as you American's say – is not on the up and up."

With lazy eyes, Della says, "I assure you that it's real."

"Does your fiancé know about Aubrey?"

"I think we've gotten far enough off topic."

Yule clears his throat. "Our main concern with promoting you, is that we'd soon lose you to marriage, like Natalia. The principal dancer is the face of the company. We can't have dancers rotating in and out of that role like a turnstile; it's only effective with tenure. You may think you can marry rich and continue to dance, but I say you can't be both Misty Copeland and Kim Kardashian. You have to choose. You, like most women, will likely choose the path of ease." He raises a palm as if to halt for a new thought. "I cannot imagine what could possibly warrant a fake engagement, but do enlighten me. If it is *not* real, it works in your favor, in regards to your promotion."

Della says, "So basically you're saying you need me to need the money."

Yule checks his watch. "Ah, the time. Excusez-moi, I vill let you get back to your… fiancé, Mademoiselle." Yule pivots and walks away.

Della enters the room and backs against the door, her head shaking.

Miles approaches, "You a'ight?"

Della's smile isn't so much a smile at all. "I messed up."

"How?"

She comes off of the door and paces in. "Yule baited me, and I fell for it."

"If you didn't outright tell him, he's just guessing."

"He wants me to admit that the engagement is fake, in order to give me the promotion."

Miles droops in misery. "So, you wanna tell him."

Della stops pacing. "Why are we doing this anyway?"

"Aw shit," Miles drops on the edge of the bed, looking down at his hands in his lap.

"No really?" Della stoops in front of him. "You concocted some story just to win an argument with Pop, and now we have to go through all this?"

Miles averts his eyes. "It's deeper than that."

Della's hands slide to her hips. "Just tell Pop you lied. What does it matter, now that you've got Yule at the business table. Free yourself."

Miles stands. "No, you wanna free *your* self."

"This is my life's dream, to become only the second black principal dancer of a major company, so yeah… You want me to put you before that?" She then puts a finger up and says, "Hold that thought. I gotta pee." Della hurries to the bathroom, hikes her skirt up and sits, leaving the door ajar to continue the conversation.

Miles seeing the cracked door as an invitation, walks in.

"Miles! What do you think you're doing?"

"What part of you haven't I seen already?"

Della allows it, but not without sucking her teeth; her dress scrunched around her waist and her shoes turned inward at the base of the toilet. "Beautiful in here, isn't it? The space… Look at that tub."

"What I'm trying to tell you, Della, is that I can't tell Pop. There're some things you don't understand."

"If there's some things I don't understand, Miles, that's on you." Della sighs and trickles. Miles chuckles. Della cuts her eyes and says, "That's why I didn't want you in here."

Miles tames his laughter with a sigh and says, "Listen, the *real* reason why Pop and I fell out was because of a woman. She was a corporate spy and I was her mark."

"What the…"

"We were at Churchill Downs, nothing but billionaires in the room. She was a Botox queen on the arm of James Jones, but she couldn't take her eyes off me. She was busty… had the waistline of a paint can–"

"–Spare me the details."

"To make a long story short, she and I, we dealt with each other one night, but she stole some documents. Next thing you know, James Jones's old ass is beating us to the new site we'd discovered."

Della, now washing her hands at the sink, eyes Miles's reflection and says, "You said you and Pop fell out over a loan. You lied to me."

"If that's the foxhole you choose to stand in, versus realizing that I was protecting my privacy after it was once compromised, this'll frame how I see you going forward."

Della pivots, meets him with a glare and then walks out of the bathroom, as if she's done.

Miles doesn't follow right away, but when he does come out of the bathroom, Della is in the middle of the bedroom, waiting to unleash these words: "Instead of lying, Miles, you could've told me there's some parts to the story you'd rather not discuss – right or wrong?"

"And create intrigue around the thing I want to keep secret? Let you piece together your own assumptions?"

Della approaches but not brazenly. She walks right into his chest and listens to it, her arms wrapped around the man. "I'm not judging you, Miles. I'm just saying that in that moment I thought we were being open and honest. Now, I'm learning that that moment was not everything I believed it to be."

Miles looks down. They're face to face, but far apart, emotionally. Miles, slowly and gently pries Della's arms from around him, as if escaping the coils of a snake. "I done spent too much time explaining myself. We have a deal in place. Either you keep your end, or you don't," Miles says and walks away, heading for the den.

Della's heart for this man pours empty like a vial of sand. "That's how you want it?"

Miles looks back and says, "I think maybe we let our imaginations get away from us." He goes into the den and closes the door behind him.

Della and Miles keep to their separate rooms as the minute hand travels the clockface. Miles is in the den, huddled over his laptop, finetuning his business proposal. Della stays in the bedroom resisting the urge to storm in and give him a piece of her mind. Miles was so cold with her that she fears this rift is as solid as the door that separates them.

Della lowers into a sitting chair by a window, just now feeling the thousands of miles between here and home. The window offers a view of the estate, but through that view, she looks inward and back in time, thinking about she and Miles's time together; that magical first night, the lovemaking, the laughs and the intimate conversations they've had in two weeks leading up to this trip. Della can't deny now that she had indeed fallen for him; otherwise, she wouldn't be so beset with grief.

Was she naïve to think that, ultimately, she mattered more to Miles than their arrangement? Her head shakes no. She blames Miles for leading her on. He made her believe he wanted to explore the possibility of a relationship. Out of the same mouth that said *If it feels real, it is real,* he now says, *We let our imaginations get away from us?* Della huffs, mocking such a notion, and yet it's her imagination that keeps feeding her scenes of reconciliation. If she would just walk through that door and let him see her tear glistened eyes, maybe it would soften his heart. Maybe he takes her in his arms and let the tenderness of a kiss reveal his true feelings and discredit his words. Surely what would ensue, is some crazy makeup sex, passion burning on the fuel of such combustible elements as regret, longing, and the resurfacing of emotional pain only to be consummated into a newer, stronger bond.

Della gets up. She runs a hand back through her hair, as if wiping thoughts out of her mind. She can't go in there, realistically. She's too afraid of letting Miles know that he has that level of power over her, nor could she bear the possible rejection.

Della examines her ghost reflection in the window and doesn't know what to do with herself. She walks over to the bed, abouts face and falls back, as stiff as a wrapped mummy but when her back hits the mattress, she thrashes momentarily, pounding the bed with her fists and the heels of her kicking feet. She snaps out of it and sits up, panting and saying between breaths, "I can't believe I'm so gone like this. This is *me*." She notices herself in the dresser mirror and goes to it. She studies herself with hands on hips, twisting from the waist. She fills herself with a deep breath, galvanizing all her magic, but she's such a mess over Miles that the thing she declares to herself in the mirror comes out sounding like a question. "You got this?"

Sick of herself, Della gets to work to distract her heart. She opens her suitcase and begins putting clothes away in the dresser and the closet.

She hears footsteps; it's Miles approaching the door that separates the bedroom and den. Hurriedly, Della pulls out some lacy lingerie, so that when Miles opens the bedroom door, he sees her examining the lingerie and saying, "Won't be needing *this*."

Miles says, "They say dinner's at seven. Hopefully that's enough time for you to get whatever this is out of your system, and leave the attitude here."

Della glances over a shoulder to see who the hell Miles thinks he's talking to, but just that quick, Miles closes the door to deny a response. "This negro done bumped his head," Della marches toward the door, but two steps in, the door opens again.

Miles adds, "By the way, we're not gone sit up here and pretend like I can't have you when I want."

Della goes to walk him down, saying, "Bro, you are *not* all that!" Miles waits, as if wanting all the smoke, but as soon as Della gets close, he slams the door dead in her face. Della tries the knob but it's locked. Out of frustration, she kicks the door then hops on one foot in agony. She hops over to the bed where she sits and massages her foot. She yells, loud enough to be heard in the den, "You have *no* idea what you just started, Miles!" Then in an odd twist, Della starts laughing. She starts laughing so uncontrollably, she has to muffle it with a pillow. She laughs not simply for the audacity of this man declaring he can have her when he wants, then slamming the door in her face, but for her grand relief that heartbreak is averted.

Obviously, Miles regrets what he'd said earlier, Della thinks. Maybe behind that door, he was sitting in the den with a heavy heart. And maybe it's not really in a man like Miles to come to her with his heart in his hand. What he said was unbelievably arrogant, but maybe arrogance is part of his love language, but as far as feelings are concerned, if he wants to play chicken and see who breaks first, then two can play at that game.

Chapter 14
Two Can Play

Got me messed up," Della says in the mirror, as she fastens her earrings. Her hair is up, neatly parted sections bobby pinned in a pompadour updo. Della puckers in the mirror. Her new lipstick, red as maraschino cherries, is *straight-popping*. Della profiles with a photo smile, then switches personas for her sexy drip; she's feeling herself. She's also feeling her dress, a no frills, vintage emerald green gown that she holds against her breast with one hand as the other hand reaches behind her for the zipper that she can't seem to reach. She goes to the den for help.

Miles – on sight – gulps air.

Gotcha, Della thinks.

"You alright," Miles asks, with a smirk.

Della matches his smirk. "Why wouldn't I be?" She aboutsface in front of him. "Zip me please?"

Miles obliges. "Stunning," floats out on a breath of awe.

Della looks back only so she can turn away in sass. "Thank you." She whisks away to the bedroom, trailing this sweet floral aroma, courtesy of Givenchy.

Miles is talkative, all of a sudden, throwing his voice through the open door while he ties his tie. "I wanna make it to dinner on time," he says from the other room. "Pop is gonna break the news about the oil drying up… Brooke already knows and she's salty because Pop's going with my proposal instead of hers."

Della, from the other room, entertains his chatter with lasses faire feedback, "Mm-hmm… Uh huh… Sure…" All the while, she grabs her purse and begins quietly backing out of their suite, closing the door oh so gently.

Della takes to the hallway with a sinister smirk in her cheek, wishing she could see the look on Miles's face when he realizes he's been talking to himself. "Wanna be petty? I'll show you petty."

She hesitates. It dawns on her that she could run into Yule without Miles by her side; nevertheless, Della goes downstairs on a scouting mission. She recalls, from their brief tour, a ballroom where maybe she can practice in the early mornings if she can clear it with staff.

Della walks clear across the main dining room, her internal compass telling her the ballroom must be on the other side, but turns out, it's not. Della finds herself near the kitchen heading into unauthorized space.

Sage exits the kitchen's double doors, to Della's surprise. "Miss Sage," calls Della, as she closes in to greet her. "They got you working?"

Sage gives a look that nearly drops Della. She says, "You should know better."

"I'm sorry, I just saw you coming out of the kitchen and assumed…"

"You're a bit early. Where's Miles?"

Sage has a noticeable glitch. Her smile seems pulled over a frown. Della explains, "I was actually trying to see if I can use the ballroom to practice in the mornings…" Della's words fade away as she realizes how they're being received.

Sage seems to expect the future wife of her billionaire son to reveal that she's only kidding. "Practice?"

"With ballet, muscle memory is everything… so even the most difficult techniques remain second nature, so when I perform, I can focus on telling the story."

"And while you're busy with ballet, who will be acting as Miles's wife?"

Della, jarred by the question replies, "With all due respect Miss Sage, I *may* retire as a wife, but since I'm still a fiancé, I must practice to avoid injury."

"You just said it was for telling the story."

"That too. I just don't want to end up like our lead dancer, Natalia, who got so wrapped up in her relationship that she was skipping on practice, then suffered a career-ending Achilles tear," Della says, to a Sage who clearly isn't listening, but only awaiting her turn to speak.

"Hear me well, Della," says Sage. "You will become what you prepare for. Ready yourself for a future as Miles's wife and it will be so. Preparing a plan B, is choosing it."

Della allows a moment of contemplation, as if the logic is sinking in. "Never thought about it like that."

"There's a lot you haven't thought about; trust me. Why don't you join me tomorrow at my spa appointment at eleven, so we can talk. I'll have them pencil you in."

"I'd be honored. Thank you, Miss Sage."

"Just Sage."

"Well, Sage, I'd be remised not to mention how much I appreciate you and your family. Everyone has been very gracious to me."

Sage draws back. "Don't count your chickens."

Candidly, Della reveals, "I gotta tell ya, I thought you all would've had a slew of servants on your heels, toting your purse dogs… but you all seem so down to earth."

The whole time Della was talking, she noticed, behind Sage, a black woman, not much younger than Sage, who had exited the kitchen and has now caught up to them. Della leans and waves.

"Sorry to interrupt," the woman says. With a thumb back over her shoulder, she tells Sage, "You might wanna come see this."

Sage says, "Carol, this is Miles's fiancé, Della. Della? Meet Carol."

Della extends a handshake. "Pleased to meet you, Miss Carol. I don't hear an accent. How long have you been living in France?"

Carol smiles quietly, as if would be more fitting for Sage to respond. Sage says, "She's with us. I had to put her on a separate flight–"

"–Wait, is this auntie?" There's a slight resemblance.

"She's *not* auntie. She's Carol," says Sage, who seems clearly peeved. She then politely sends Carol back, assuring she'll be right behind her. Once Carol is out of hearing range, Sage positions herself square with Della to say, "Carol is my personal chef who I flew in, on a separate flight, all the way to Paris because I don't trust anyone else to prepare my blue fin tuna. Still think I'm so *down to earth?* It's not the compliment you think it is. To me it sounds like you're calling me basic, and there is nothing basic about me, toots."

Toots?! Della is so triggered by Sage's inconceivable rudeness, hair raises on the back of Della's neck. She's a moment away from saying F-it and throwing away her quarter of a million-dollar deal with Miles just to go off on his mother, but Della finds it in herself to go with diplomacy, "My apologies. I didn't mean to offend."

"Then you go find Miles, and find your way back to the dining room on his arm and on time, mm-kay?"

Della ditches plan A, to slap Sage's face clean, into a dust-cloud of makeup, but without a plan B Della just stands firmly in stalemate, because she'd sooner mop up the Atlantic Ocean than let someone dismiss her so coldly.

"Got something to say," says Sage. "Cat got your tongue? Whatever you have to say, save it for tomorrow, Della. As gorgeous as you look this evening, I need you out of my sight. Be gone." Sage shoos Della with two back-flicks of her hand.

With a stiff upper lip, Della says, "Thank you for the compliment." She walks away burning. If anger were flames, she'd be engulfed in it like an action stuntman. She's convinced that over the course of this week, Sage will be the test for how much disrespect a quarter of a million dollars is worth.

Della retraces her path towards the suite, canceling her ambition to secure a venue for practice. Going against Sage's advice might open the door to more hazing.

Della checks her phone. There's a text from Miles, *Y u playin?* Prior to her encounter with Sage, the message would've tickled Della, but now it only offers a new target for her anger. She looks up from her phone and there is the man himself, Miles, in a cream-colored suit with a brandy tie and pocket hanky.

"So you got jokes, huh," he says, as he catches up.

"Miles? I'm *not* in the mood."

Miles thinks her attitude is about him. He dips over a single clap held to his chest. "Oh you mad? Is that why you slipped out of the room?"

Della sighs and says, "If I slap the hell out of your mother, do I still get to keep this ring?"

"What'd she do," Miles asks, then chuckles over a fist.

"Sage is not a real person. No one is that rude. And I find it funny how she's so nice in front of you and Pop." Della then transcribes the interaction nearly line by line, punctuating with a hand to her breast saying, "And that lady looked me right in the face and said, 'Be gone'? I swear my pimp hand was itching," Della says, obvious kidding. She raises one pledged hand to say, "Forgive me for saying, Miles, but your mother is toxic."

"Toxic, you say?" Miles rubs his chin and says, "The thing about toxic behavior is the person developed it, at some point, as a way to protect themselves."

As they head for the dining room, Miles uses the long walk to explain how Sage, as a child, had a debilitating stutter. Although she spoke fluent French, Creole, and Patois, only English made her look like a severe Tourette's case. She was bullied in school, and her hot-tempered Haitian parents treated her like a bad seed. Miles reckons that his mother was triggered when Della called Carol auntie before Sage had a chance to fully introduce them. "Momma ain't never liked being interrupted. She reverts to the little girl being dismissed as a handicap."

"That's why she took such pleasure in dismissing *me*." They walk a few more paces before Della says, "That may be her reason, but it's no reason for me accept disrespect; she'll still catch these hands."

Miles sucks his teeth and walks ahead, stiff as a pole.

"What," Della laughs.

He turns and walks backward in pace. "Always talkin' about some hands." He takes her hand. "Can't much palm a baseball. Who you gone hurt with this?"

Della glances around, speaking like a ventriloquist, through a smile of embarrassment. "Stop playing Miles. We're supposed to be acting important."

Miles looks her up and down as he takes her side again, but keeps her hand, interlocking the fingers.

Della glances at their held hands then back at Miles.

Miles replies, "My peoples ain't seen us hold hands or kiss or nothing, yet."

Playfully, Della bumps him with a hip and says, "If you want my affection, Miles, just say that." Her attempt to resist blushing, only accentuates it.

Miles tries to subdue a smile of his own.

Della takes a calming breath and says, "Gotta prepare myself to face your mother again. Maybe she'll be different in front of your father."

Miles's eyes slice over. "If anybody's toxic, it's Pop."

Chapter 15
When It Feels Real

The weary eyes around the dinner table says they've heard this speech a hundred times or more.

Pop starts his speech in the sixties during the second oil boom, when a small-time Illinois farmer by the name of Silas McKinnon was digging an irrigation well but discovered a different kind of well when a geyser of crude oil burst up from the ground and shot him six feet in the air. Unlike other landowners who'd struck, Silas refused to sell out to the Texas oil companies that became giants during the first oil boom in the thirties and forties. Silas dared to do the impossible – to build his own oil rig. He sold off his farm assets for the down payment on a bank loan that was backed by the value of the underground lake of oil. With farming taken away as a means to make a living, Silas took odd jobs and the family lived in poverty while awaiting the construction of the rig. With automobile production and petroleum consumption approaching new all-time highs, Silas's gamble paid off and the McKinnons leaped four social classes in only the first year of operation, thus, the dynasty was formed.

In the nineties, shortly after Pop succeeded his father as CEO, Pop took his own big risk, against Silas's advice. Pop spent millions on acres of land and equipment to farm corn. He formed a badly marketed liquor label, although spirits was never the vision, nor was he getting back to the McKinnon's farming roots. Pop was betting that renewable fuels was the future. He lost hundreds of thousands per year until that future arrived in the Energy Policy Act of 2005, which mandated that oil companies blend biofuels into their fuel supply. Since then, they've raked in billions from the ethanol arm of the company alone.

Pop pauses his story and gazes around the table. Without so much as a segue, he drops the bombshell. "And now analysts say that our Richland County oil field is nearing its end of life."

Eliza and Dutch eye each other. Madison looks up from the phone in her lap and smooths her hair behind an ear.

Pop queues Brooke to come up and say a few words.

Brooke stands in his place at the head of the table. Brooke is so unassuming, one would never guess she's the Chief Operating Officer for a multi-billion-dollar corporation who'd earned her stripes on an oil rig, in a hardhat and skirt. She begins, "Sonar images show a cavernous bottom, so hydraulic fracturing can extend the life of the site a few more years at best; otherwise, by 2025, the Lieber scale of the operational burden versus the declining profits will level." Brook surveys her listeners before resuming. "And what that means *Madison* is that, as a company, we'll be leaving Illinois altogether. A couple years ago, we had eyes on our last viable site in Illinois, but we fumbled the bag. And when I say *we*, I mean Miles." In good humor, she puts up a front-facing fist and says, "Luh you bro… We don't have the margins of a BP or Exxon, so we're super selective when it comes to new ventures. Aside from the Illinois site where the rug was yanked out from under us, our field research shows the most promising ventures that offer traditional extraction methods *and* meet our risk and sustainability thresholds are in North Dakota. But as I said, we're a small oil company, but our bioethanol component makes us a big *energy* company." Brooke, without looking down at any notes, gives a seminar-worthy explanation of how The Paris Agreement to lower emissions is sixty percent commitment to private sector companies, like themselves, and since there's only one other company, located in Dublin, that has an efficient model for industrial sized mechanical trees, Vanguard Energy could, more likely than not, become a global leader, and whomever is sitting CEO of Vanguard, in the next few years, could potentially become regarded as the world's next Jeff Bezos or Elon Musk. Brooke then explains how pivotal this week is, which gives them all the more reason to be gracious to Yule and his staff.

Pop gets up for final words but Brooke stops him and goes off-script. "Our alternative is more drilling and undertaking the rigorous work of securing permits and construction… So Miles?" Brook sighs. "I'm not gone lie, I've got strong feelings about you being both the problem and the solution, but I really hope you can pull off this deal and take over my operational role because I can't do North Dakota." There's a heavy silence brought on by disbelief. Pop is as heartbroken as he is shocked. Brooke imparts, "In a couple months I won't even be able to board a plane… Because I'm pregnant."

Brooke and her husband Omari, who stayed home with their one child, had given up on having a second, but now pregnant in her mid-thirties, the family surrounds Brooke with love, tears, and thanksgiving to an on-time God.

Soon they settle in and all the attention is on Brooke, which makes it easy for Della to avoid Sage.

Pop claps for a server, "Garcon?" He then leans back in his chair to whisper in the waiter's ear. Soon the waiter returns with their top bottles, made on this very estate.

After a few glasses of wine, dinner is served and the family is engaged in conversation, except for Miles and Della who seem so exclusively into each other. Miles's hand is obviously on Della's thigh under the table. Flirtatiously, he leans and whispers something naughty, which prompts Della to shush him and giggle. Della stabs an ice-poached oyster with her fork, dips it in sauce that's held in the pedal of a tulip. She then brings the fork to Miles's mouth. Della imagines herself in the place of the oyster as Miles teases it with his tongue, and then slowly sucks the mollusk through puckered lips.

Sage jabs Pop with an elbow and says, "Mick, do you see your son?"

Miles and Della periscope, holding laughter.

Pop explains, "They're just young and in love, Sage."

Miles wipes his mouth with a napkin and says, "We always feed each other, ma. That's our thing."

To Pop, Sage replies, "What do I expect? If they're carrying on like this, I expect grandchildren right away."

Pop is with her on this one. "Five adult children and just two grands… one living in Bermuda that we see only a few times a year… one more on the way, God willing."

Dutch chimes in with a hand raised. "Actually, Liza and me 'bout to give you one."

No one even looks at Dutch. Miles and Della, across the table from Sage and Pop, are locked in on each other.

Sage says, "Don't waste your breath, Mick. This one (meaning Della) isn't thinking about children until she's done with ballet."

Della attempts to speak the moment Sage starts. Della raises two palms. "Sorry, I didn't mean to interrupt."

Sage says, "If you have something to say, say it."

Della says, "I learned from the last time I cut you off."

Sage frowns. "Say what?"

Pop intercedes, "Sage… Now is not the time."

Sage looks at Pop as if he's a bug she's fixing to squash. "Now's not the time for what? We're just talking."

Miles says, "Chill, ma."

Sage hardens her glare. "I have questions. You see, not only have *you* never mentioned her, the groundskeepers, nor pool cleaner never laid eyes on this young lady. Nor the maid, who hasn't come across any evidence of a woman until the last couple weeks. Another thing: when did you have time to court this young lady? You spent two straight months in Illinois, and even when you returned to New Jersey, you may have been working remotely, but tirelessly, late every day, doing your penance… So tell me son, where did you all find the time?"

This is not one of the inquiries that Miles and Della had rehearsed for. Miles can feel Della's panic through his hand on her thigh under the table, so he beats Della to a response, so she doesn't do something wacky like the time she quoted Usher. Miles says, "You interrogated the staff?"

"This is all too sudden. Why shouldn't I look into it."

"But ma—"

"—Miles." Della turns in her chair to face Miles. "Your mother is concerned, as any mother would be. She doesn't know that I began falling for you before I had any idea who you were. I wasn't looking for anything. I was already living my dream. Who knew that I would meet someone like you, who is so amazing to me, that you so suddenly changed the course of my life." Under some new revelation, Della's eyes widen. "With you, my dreams suddenly opened up to invite… more. I know that you opening your heart to me wasn't easy for you, but…"

Miles touches her face. "That's where you're wrong, babe. That was the easiest thing ever in life. Telling you was the hard part."

Della's head shakes in silence; this performance is intended to run away from the question, but looking back, Della realizes she'd run herself smack into emotions that's as real as a concrete wall. She adds, "If any words spoken at this table echo some sort of doubt you may have about me, let me say it to you now. As your wife, what you desire is of the utmost importance to me. If you want children sooner rather than later, I will meet the desire of your heart the way you meet mine. Because I love you, Miles."

Miles clears a tear from Della's cheek, and touches his forehead to hers.

Della, overwhelmed with emotion, gets out of her chair. "Excuse me, everyone," she says, and leaves.

Miles mean-mugs his mother as he drops his napkin on his plate, then he goes after Della.

The whole table looks around in silence, except for Madison, sniffling and dabbing the corners of her eyes with a dinner napkin, the other hand shaking a finger at the two empty seats. "If the love don't hit like that, I don't want it."

Eliza, clutching the chakra stones on her necklace, looks up at her mother and says, eerily, "That was real."

Della hurries across the dining room, enroute to the ladies room. Yule, also hurrying across the dining room with a box of cigars, nearly bumps into Della. He fixes his mouth to apologize, but Della blasts, in a single, vicious bark, *"Get!"*

Next, Miles in hot pursuit, comes streaking across Yule's path, shrugging and smiling awkwardly.

Miles arrives at the ladies' room just as the door shuts behind Della. He puts his back to the wall and says, "That was good, Della. Hell, you had even me convinced, babe… Babe?" Miles knocks and calls Della by name. The way she responds, *What*, in a broken note, tells Miles she's falling apart in there.

"Will you come out and talk to me?"

Della replies. "I can't go back to that table."

"Fine," Miles says. "Let's go for a walk."

Della comes out, takes Miles's hand and they leave.

Chapter 16
Fortunato

At the dinner table, Pop is doing damage control. "…I tried to restore everyone's faith in Miles by saying that *he* was one who secured this business meeting with Yule, but it was actually Della. Yule called *Della* – not Miles's." Pop looks around the table at Eliza, Dutch, Brooke but stops on Sage. "So, whether you think she's genuine or not, we should at least, in the spirit of gratitude, make her feel comfortable. Don't put her on the hotseat as if she's some skank. Got me?"

Sage protests, "Mick, all I was trying to say was–"

"–Sage," Pop says, in a warning tone. "I'm trying my best not to raise my voice." And that ends the discussion.

Yule arrives, saying, "I just thought I'd stop by and check on everyone. Enjoying the meal?"

Brooke answers for everyone by kissing her fingertips like a French chef.

"I heard the good news about the baby on the way. I brought cigars for the gentlemen." Yule takes two cigars from the box and hands them to Pop. "The other is for Miles, when he returns."

Dutch exaggeratedly clears his throat.

Yule swivels to Dutch. "Oh? Am I mistaken?" Yule, with a look of foreign bewilderment, hands a cigar across the table to Dutch.

Next Yule turns to Pop. "Monsieur Mick, my staff tells me you requested our premium wine selections." He does a finger wag and tongue-clicks for shame. "You should have found me directly. Come see my private stock, and maybe we can get a head start on business."

Pop leans toward Sage, knowing there's face to save and emotional ground cover, after having threatened to raise his voice. Pop says, "I won't be long babe." His wife is stone. Pop playfully tries to kiss Sage's face, as an alley-oop for her to reject him and call it even.

"Gone now, Mick." Sage swerves away, refusing to crack a smile until Pop is gone and then Sage is reassuring the others of who's really the boss in their marriage.

Yule leads Pop down a long hallway and into what appears to be a small sanctuary. Yule narrates, "During the great plague, it was too dangerous for the town to gather at church. Many constructed shrines and had Sabbath in their homes." Yule swirls a finger at Pop and says, "Turn around please?"

"Say what?" A confused Pop only looks back.

"All the way around."

Pop turns his back to Yule, who then pulls a porcelain figurine of Simon Peter with his sword raised to cut off the ear of Malchus. "Come," says Yule.

To Pop's astonishment, the wall opens to the sound of grinding rock. Yule leads Pop down another hallway to a thick wooden door mounted with a kite shield that has the picture of a golden foot crushing a snake, but the snake's head is turned back, biting the heel in retaliation.

Pop doesn't ask, but Yule senses his curiosity. "This is our retired coat of arms." Yule jabs the door with an iron key and turns it.

Pop gathers that Yule's family, the Montresors, is not represented by the human foot, but rather the snake with its fang sunken into the heel. There is a caption engraved, *Nemo me impune lacessit.*

"Our modern coat of arms is the Poseidon trident, for the many ships we've docked at the Bay of Biscay. We amassed our wealth as transporters of… goods."

There's long hallway with exposed structural beams disappearing in darkness like a coal mine. Hesitantly, Pop says, "Just to be sure, we are down here for wine, right?"

"The very best, monsieur."

They walk the downward slope into darkness, the grit of shoes echoing far beyond their limited sight. There's a hint of limestone and something earthy. Yule takes an electric torch from the wall holster. Pop notices how, in the distance, the walls turn to cobblestone, but as they advance, the cobblestone clusters begin to look strange, too uniform in shape and size. As they draw near, the torch's halo reveals – not cobblestone, but skulls! Pop screams, "What the!" He bolts.

"Monsieur!"

Pop stops at the torch's boundary of light, facing a darkness as thick as smoke. Yule's hand is stretched towards him.

"Monsieur! Have you not seen catacombs before?"

"Not without warning! You could've said something!"

"The shrine… The coat of arms… They meant nothing to you?"

Pop shuffles in frustration. "Man, how much further we got to go?"

"Not much. Not much at all."

Pop follows Yule through centuries of Montresor remains. "The plague hit us hard, as you can see, how this area is much denser with bones. Anyway," Yule says, "About this proposal. My partners and I see it is very attractive. The numbers, in regard to the emission reduction component, speak for themselves. But numbers, Monsieur Mick, is not the only concern of my partners."

"Here we go," sighs Pop, with stirring recognition.

Yule says, "We've done a little homework."

Pop nods. "Of course."

"Your daughter Corine–"

"–You mean Brooke. Corine doesn't work for Vanguard Energy."

"Two of the nations that Corine represents, Guadalupe and Martinique, are French territories."

Pop draws back like a snake tensed to strike. "Look, if you expect me to backdoor my own daughter, we may as well turn back right now."

"It's French resentment, Monsieur Mick. Businesses from French Territories become increasingly vindictive in their dealings."

Pop's arms float out to his sides. "Man, I'm from Dunlap, Illinois."

Yule raises a finger. "But the fact that you still haven't mentioned that your wife is born of Haitian immigrants is concerning."

Pop's head dips. "You're kidding."

"Haiti just paid off a debt to France that has crippled their currency since the reign of our King Charles the 10th, and it'll take their economy another hundred years to recover. Haitian trade partners raise their rates as a form of reparations, it seems."

Pop's arms fall slack to his sides. "Enough with the shit, okay. If what you want is for me to buy my way in, you don't have to concoct some excuse. My question to you is: how much?"

"So impatient, monsieur." Yule comes to a stop at a wine barrel mounted in recess of stone. "First, we drink."

Pop's eyes flair. "I ain't drinkin' that shit. I may not have French resentment, but I damn sure got drinking-around-dead-bodies-and-pestilence, resentment."

Yule takes two shot glasses from his breast pocket. He uses an odd shaped key to release a cylinder of wine so the barrel stays airtight. From this cylinder, Yule fills the glasses. After a swirl under his nose, Yule downs his shot with a grimace. "It gets sweeter with time, yet I must warn you that these old barrels gives an aftertaste of tree sap." Yule fills the second shot glass and extends it to Pop, who has no intention of taking it. "You must," Yule says. "…If we are to do business."

Pop takes it, with a scowl. "This has got to be the foolest thing I've ever done." He downs the shot and has a coughing fit. "No offense, Yule, but what the *hell* is this?"

Yule refills Pop's glass. "This, monsieur Mick, is a near three-hundred-year-old cask of Amontillado. Right behind it, embedded in this limestone wall is the bones of someone who is *not* a Montressor. He is a fool who went by the name of Fortunato."

Pop downs his second glass and shudders.

Yule, while refilling the glasses again, continues, "Fortunato merely insulted a Montresor, who then got him intoxicated off of this same barrel and then constructed a brick wall around him which became Fortunato's grave." Yule hands Pop another glass.

Pop now takes it suspectly.

"I brought you here," says Yule. "So you will better understand my side of the negotiations, and because the vengeance enacted upon Fortunato is quite relevant to our situation."

Pop looks up from his third glass. "Relevant how?"

"You have a traitor in your camp."

Pop's brow wrinkles, shadowy in torch light. "You alright, brotha? You good? Because you sound, to me, like somebody who's off their meds, man."

"This is inconceivable to you? Even after Miles had been compromised by a woman before?"

"Wait." Pop cancels his swig. "Who told you that?"

"The traitor, monsieur. Della brought that intel to me, desperate to win my favor. She'll do anything to be promoted to principal dancer – anything but *one* thing."

"That being?"

Yule leaks a sinister laugh.

Pop downs his drink and says, "What if there was no purpose to why Della shared that with you. What if she was just talking, like women are known to do. I'm inclined to believe that she loves my son, and didn't intend any harm to him or me."

"The engagement is fraudulent. Della is involved with a doctor who feeds her addiction to pain killers."

"Addiction to pain killers!"

"Oui monsieur. And he too can attest that Della and Miles only met the night Miles gave me his business card."

Pop thinks out loud. "Miles lied about that? But why? It makes no sense."

Yule inquires, "When did Miles say they met?"

Pop visits the memory, the morning he found a woman's things in Miles's living room and remembers. "He didn't say, actually. He side-stepped the question."

"Then he is not lying. Maybe the engagement is real to *him*. Miles is a victim."

Pop counters, "But Miles isn't the type to fall fast. Even with that Lori girl who had all these famous men falling head over heels for her… her magic didn't work on Miles."

"It's Della, I'm telling you. She is… intense. Her grace, her feminine energy… She's quite a captivating."

Pop downs another shot. The taste spurs an epiphany, it seems, how as soon as the glass leaves Pop's lips, he's asking, with a bitter face, "Why're you so focused on Della, anyway? What the hell she done to you?"

"Well, one day I looked in on a dance rehearsal. I was being quite social. She mistook my kind words as improper, and she slapped my face." Yule turns his head to illustrate. "My head spun so fast, the lights smeared across my vision. That, Monsieur Mick, cannot stand."

Pop imparts, "She's but a young lady. You're *how* old?"

"This young lady that is deceiving your son. She must be humbled."

Pop frowns. "Just let it go, brotha."

Yule turns from the waist. "Let it go? I bring you here behind the shield of my ancestors, the grave of Fortunato at my back, so you'd understand why I can't 'just let it go.' Vengeance will be mine."

"How? The good Lord put it up for sale, or somethin'?"

"I have a perfect plan, but I'll need your assistance."

Pop leans away. "You just said vengeance is yours, now wanna split it with me? You don't need help. Deny Della the promotion out of spite, or slap the hell out of *her*."

"Bah," Yule swats the air. "Cheek for cheek is not revenge. The consequence must be graver than the offense. And there must be an element of irony. The very thing she sought to deny, I must make her submit."

Pop pours another shot. "You say you had a perfect plan. I'm gone shut up and hear you out, so we can get outta here and let these dead folks rest."

Yule sighs and says, "First, I need you to expose Della, so Miles can break off the engagement."

Pop perks up. "Oh, I was gone do that, regardless. My son with an addict?" He shudders at the thought.

"Initially – as far as the bribe is concerned – I was thinking one point five million. Half a million for each of my two colleagues, and then myself, to secure all three of the required recommendations, but now there is a change. Since Della is here–

"–Here because of *you*. You got some nerve, acting as if her presence is some accident. On that first day when we talked, as soon I mentioned that Della was accompanying us on the family retreat, all of a sudden you become impatient, couldn't wait. We had to do the retreat in Paris or no deal?" Pop looks down in his glass; his head shakes. "All along *this* was your motivation? Jerking my family around because you got slapped?"

Yule relents, "I know I'm taking this to the extreme, but I'm too set in my ways to do it any differently. So, here's the plan: Once you expose her to Miles and he dumps her, she'll be looking for any money grab she can get. Instead of my half million, you can save yourself a lot of money by making Della a cash offer to… be with me."

"Uh-uh. I won't take part in exploiting a young lady – addict or not. I will however, talk some sense into Miles–"

"–On that point, then, we adjourn. You say you will convince Miles to end the relationship. Good! Because if Miles does not break from her, then the money, and even a promotion, will be rendered ineffective."

Pop, with a suspicious eye, asks, "What's wrong with you offering the money ya damn self?"

"Because that would give her the power to have me removed from the Manhattan Dance Company's board of directors. So, the money, and the proposition, must come from someone else." Yule turns sinister, adding, "Vanguard Energy's financials looks good from the outside, but judging by how you so suddenly rearranged your whole family retreat, I suspect an internal crisis. I believe that securing this partnership *is*, perhaps, important enough for you to 'exploit a young lady'."

Yule collects the glasses and the torch. All along he's still speaking but Pop's mind is elsewhere. Pop, wondering what he's gotten himself into, stares blankly at the wall, his vision coming into focus, squarely fixed on a skull with dark eye sockets and a gate of teeth, a Montresor, centuries dead, smiling at him, mocking him.

135

PART IV

Chapter 17
No More Games

Night bears down on the horizon, the distant mountainside rich with bold font shadows. Miles and Della stroll the grounds of the Montressor estate along an asphalt public trail through the vineyard. Della walks carefully, so not to sweep the ground with the hem of her gown.

Silence is pregnant with an argument awaiting a spark, which Della finally realizes that she must be the one to provide it. "Let's just go back," she says — and to be sure that her displeasure not be mistaken for mere inspiration, she adds, "You're not talking about nothing, anyway."

Miles peers down at Della. "Sometimes talk gets in the way. Sometimes it's better for both to shut the fuck up."

Della long-steps and turns to confront Miles with a finger pointing in his face. "You better watch your mouth, with me."

Miles doesn't so much as lean to avoid a possible poke in the eye. "Did you hear what I said, or did you only hear the last part?"

"It's not what I'm hearing; it's what I'm *not* hearing."

Miles just glares and waits. The moment Della's pointing hand starts coming down, on its own volition, Miles takes the credit. "Getchya damn hand out my face." He flicks his tongue to show Della he's only kidding.

Defiantly, Della points again. "You be playing at the wrong times, Miles. It's gonna end up costing you."

"Costing me what?"

"*Me…* If that means anything to you."

Every kink of humor in Miles's face falls earnest. "You just wanna hear me say it, don't you? Isn't it obvious?" Miles takes Della's hands in his. He gazes in her eyes, a vague smile upon his lips. "You said it yourself, that once Yule agreed to meet, I had nothing to lose by telling Pop the truth about us, but… it wasn't about Pop at that point; it was more for me. It gave me a legit reason to lay eyes on you every day up to this trip; shopping, getting our lies straight… I had to make that the reason, because I desire to spend every waking minute with you, but couldn't fix my mouth to tell you; I'm not built like that."

Della's arms are around him; she looks up, stargazing in his eyes. Miles's strong jawline and brow is as chiseled as the Pyrenees mountains in the distance behind him.

Miles adds, "With that being said, you're my lady for real now. It's official."

Eyes fall closed. Their lips come together with a bundle of emotions. All uncertainties are put to rest and they're now full with wonder. Even now as they embrace under a chalky moon, they're reimagining their future into the journey of a pair. Miles breaks the kiss to study her. Della's beauty, to Miles, looks enchanted, as if she's some pointed-eared nymph who is guardian of this vineyard. Miles says, "As my lady, whatever you need, financially, I need it for you. Whatever you want, I want it for you."

This promise makes Della squeamish. "Miles, that's not what I'm here for. Look, I've always managed on my own."

"Not no more." He smiles, paternally. "Imagine me struggling and you having it to give. Would it be any different?"

Della's head shakes no as she looks with eyes that never seem to have their fill of him… her African prince, with his cream suit and dreadlocks; the castle just there in the distance, to which they'll soon return and, make love for the first time as a real couple.

"Keep the ring," Miles says.

Della looks at the ring, then looks at him. Hesitantly, she says, "You already told me I could, or do you mean…"

Miles looks around, his eyes wandering then coming back to her. "You're not gonna let me have any peace until I tell you everything that's on my heart, huh?"

Della, with lips folded in, shakes her head no.

"Let's walk," says Miles.

On their way back to the chateau, it takes him a while to begin. They're out of the vineyard and strolling the exotic garden when Miles explains how, when a man finds *the one*, he also finds himself. He will feel a pull inside of him like he's never felt before. Not once does Miles look over at Della; he looks straight ahead. "This pull I feel towards you, could tug a bus."

MILES's phone rings. It's Pop calling to report what Yule had exposed about Della. Miles's phone, however, is in the front pocket of pants that lay on the checker tiled bathroom floor at the foot of the jade-colored platform tub that has a lion's face carved on the side of it. Pop figures the message is too heavy to leave as a voicemail.

Miles and Della's shared bath sucks down the drain while they lay on the other side of the wall in bed together, Della's arms are outstretched, pinned to the bed, Miles deep inside of her. She's at the brink of tears with pleasure from slow sensuous lovemaking, so there couldn't be a more peculiar time for Miles to want to have a conversation.

"Look at me, goddess. Let me see your eyes." He hits bottom and Della's eyes spring open. "Listen to your man," he says. "I am your man, right?" He wants to hear it. Della is so lost in ecstasy that Miles must ask again.

Della bites her lip and moans. "Mmm-*hmm*."

Miles draws himself out to the pulsing tip, as if intent on denying Della more of him until she answers the next question, "Is that all I am to you?"

Della trembles and whines, "I'm almost there, baby."

"I know." Miles whispers. "I'm holding back because you're holding back."

Della, sick with yearning, bucks into him, but Miles denies her. Della gasps in frustration. "Gimme," she begs.

Miles lowers to kiss her lips, and resumes stroking ever so slowly, holding her in suspense.

"Oh Miles."

"You like that?" The stroke hits bottom again.

She claws his back. "Mm-*hmm*…"

"What you said at dinner… was that real?" Della exhales slowly as the stroke hits bottom again.

Della squirms in heat but stops when she realizes what Miles just said. Della reaches up to place a gentle hand on the side of Miles's face, as if seeing him – in a way – for the first time. "Everything I had said…" Della swallows hard, tears fill the wells of her eyes. "…was real."

Apparently, this is what Miles was waiting to hear. He picks up the pace. "Are you sure?"

Della feels herself peaking. "Oh yes! It was so real, baby. Oh my *God* it was real!" She's slingshots into orgasmic outer space; her eyes clapped shut. Della releases a yodel as she hurls past stars, meteors and nebulas, until finally, she plumets back down into her own body, lying on her back and convulsing with pelvic spasms, tears running back into her ears, but she's now cognizant enough to ask, "So, we're…" She shakes her head to cancel the question as if it's too absurd to ask.

A few moments of silence goes by. Miles says, "I know what you were about to ask." Miles now lie on his back, his eyes nearly closed just to look down at her.

"Well, earlier you told me to keep the ring… Just now, you asked if what I said at the dinner table was real, so…"

"Don't you feel it?"

She does, but Della wonders if she's under the spell of such amazing lovemaking. Della's finger traces the muscular line down the center of his chest. "We can stretch out the engagement, ya know… take our time… My grandma used to say that things put together with haste, fall apart with haste."

Miles kisses her head. "Must be a Carolina thing."

Della feels Miles's breathing change as he succumbs to sleep. Della doesn't know why she feels the need to ask, but she asks anyway. "Miles? Did you come in me?"

"Want me to?"

"No, but, did you?"

"Don't be silly babe."

Chapter 18
Alignment

Pop eases out of bed, careful not to wake Sage. The room is dark. He sets his feet in the slippers by the bed and heads toward the minifridge for a bottled water, but when he passes by the dresser, something catches his eye in the mirror. He returns to examine a cloudy, ghostly shape, perhaps a stain. Pop leans in, wipes a hand across the glass and it clears away like the condensation of steam; there's no water running in the master bath.

What's even stranger, Pop's dark silhouette does not appear in the mirror. Quietly terrified, Pop clicks on the lamp. His reflection reveals that his head is a whole clean skull with a single maggot wriggling in the nose cavity. Pop screams. His bone-faced reflection screams, in a lipless display of teeth.

Sage hurries from the bathroom and shakes Pop awake.

Pop comes to, wide-eyed but disoriented. Sage is over him in a night bonnet and facial mask with circles around her eyes. Pop mistakes her for another skull and screams again. "Dammit Sage. You scared the hell outta me."

Sage draws back. "Me? Something else got to you first, obviously. What were you dreaming about?"

"A damn skull." Pop feels his face and pinches his nose.

"Can you be more specific?"

"My face… it was a skull, Sage, a dry skull."

Sage studies her husband for a few beats, in silent interrogation.

Pop frowns, confusedly, "What is it?"

Sage asks, "What did you and Yule discuss last night?"

Pop knows he cannot tell Sage about Della being an addict; it would only justify Sage's ill treatment of her. Neither can Pop tell Sage about Yule wanting to exploit Della in order to approve the deal. Pop's existing frown tightens. "We didn't talk about anything, hardly."

Sage, with the weight of nearly forty years of marriage behind her pointed finger, accuses, "You're worried about something. You drink when you worry, and last night you were drunk as a skunk."

"From only, like four small glasses."

Sage squints harder. "You're afraid you're going to have to compromise this deal."

"You're getting all this from a dream?" Pop laughs.

Sage knows this man, and that his laughter is riddled with nerves of deception. Sage leans over Pop, setting both hands, knuckles down, on the bed. Pop is backed up against the headboard; he fondly and carefully places a kiss where the facial mask carves around Sage's lips.

"Mick," says Sage. Her head shakes with each repetition of the name. "Mick, Mick, Mick… I hope you're not about to let them push you into a lesser deal." There's a slight wonder in Sage's eyes, as if she's given to madness. "We can't risk looking grateful. This deal has to hurt them just a little bit if it's going to earn us any respect. As far as Corine and me… there are people that we'll have to face, and doors that we need to stay open for us."

Pop replies, "Our asking price still stands. But I'm not leaving anything up to chance. Yule offered a bribe, and I'm taking it, a one-point-five-million-dollar bribe."

"One point five million dollars?" Sage's hands roll palms up. "Why, that's nothing."

"Exactly," says Pop.

Sage raises up straight, pivots and resumes her morning routine. She's soon in the bathroom with the sink on, rinsing away her mask.

Pop shoves his feet into the slippers by the bed. He swipes his phone off the nightstand, goes to the den and sits on the couch next to his golfing attire, which is already ironed and laid out by Sage.

Sage enters the den, patting her face with a towel, her skin looking radiant and blessed. "Breakfast is in-suite this morning, hon. I ordered you crapes."

Pop points at his phone in dismay. "I just texted Miles to meet up early, so we can talk about this business…"

Sage takes a seat in Pop's lap. "C'mon, Mick," she whines. "You hijacked our family retreat, remember? I've looked over the itinerary and it seems that our only opportunity to spend quality time, is the night of the ball."

"Seriously?" Pop considers the oversight.

"Besides, Mick, you don't need a whole hour to tell Miles what you just told me in a few minutes…" Her mind drifts momentarily. "Unless there's something more you're not telling me."

Pop smiles sheepishly. "Miles can wait."

Sage is as happy as a girl. She kisses Pop and then holds him there by the sides of his face.

Pop then takes out his phone and turns the display to Sage. "Question. What does this say? I took a picture of it on the way out of the catacombs."

Sage squints. "Is that a snake?"

"It is," answers Pop. "See the words underneath it though? It's French."

"*Nemo me impune lacessit.* It's old. It's Latin. French wasn't always France's official language. It says, 'No one attacks me with impunity'? Or something like that."

Room service knocks and Sage hurries to the door. With Sage gone, Pop deflates in the chair. Having breakfast with Sage surrenders the only opportunity Pop had to talk to Miles. It could be messy to have the conversation on the golf course in Dutch's presence, especially when Yule's version of events is possibly lies, with the intent to secure vengeance against Della. Yule swears he was slapped over a misunderstanding, but Pop recalls meeting Della, and her characterizing Yule as a creep who was handsy with both female and male dancers, which is likely the real reason Della slapped Yule's face, Pop reckons.

In any event, entering the preliminary meeting this afternoon without executing the one item Pop agreed to, which is to expose Della to Miles, the entire deal may be at risk. This weighs heavily on Pop. His troubled head bows and rests in the grip of his hands.

MILES is already at the golf course with rented clubs when he gets Pop's text to cancel their early meeting. Miles doesn't return to Della. He unsheathes his putter and stays out on the practice greens, his brown eyes blazing with the light of the sun presiding over the hillside.

For nearly a half hour straight, Miles misses nearly every putt. His concentration is shot because his mind is stuck on last night. Miles now thinks maybe it was a bad look to discuss marriage under the intoxication of sex.

He takes a golf ball from the basket and places it on the 15ft marker. He arranges his stance; the game of golf is all about alignment. The imaginary line across the tips of his golf shoes extends parallel to the hole. The clubface is perpendicular to that imaginary line. The putter grip is aligned so that the crest on the pendulum of his swing meets the ball at its center. Miles gives the backswing a quarter turn and let his torso unwind naturally into the strike. The ball rolls alongside its morning shadow, seemingly on target, but it rims around the left side of the hole in a near miss. If one line is off, every line is off.

Miles thinks about this morning, how Della seemed overwhelmed with joy, but now revisiting their interactions in the grey of memory, Miles realizes that maybe she was just overwhelmed period – how she'd stop in the middle of getting dressed, dazed with some new epiphany. In her underwear and holding a wide-toothed comb, she stared at Miles who had one leg in a pair of plaid golfing pants. Della had then asked; *Does this mean we're going to cohabitate?* It's as if it seems a bit much for Della to move in straightaway after the proposal like a Jare and Natalia.

Miles, again remembers how, just before leaving, he saw Della staring at her mirror reflection while fondling the crucifix on her necklace. Miles came up from behind, adding himself to the mirror's frame. Della, in a low, measured tone had said, *Mister and Missus McKinnon...* and nothing more.

Miles places another ball on the marker and let the club fall relaxed in his hands. Next, he begins to study his alignment; the putter, the stance, his head tilted forward so the eyes are directly line over the ball. Miles shakes his head at the realization that he and Della are set to marry though they have yet to utter the first I love you.

Miles squints at the ball, the hole, and clubface. Sunlight casts a faint rainbow across the brush of his eyelashes. The lines can't seem to come together, so he backs away and resets his stance – you see, because love, in the beginning, is nothing more than a vague notion, and Miles believes he's committed to idea of convincing himself, for the rest of his life, that this notion about Della is right. And it *is*, Miles asserts. He knew since he first saw Della on stage in a tutu and bodice, finishing her turn in a magnificent pose, where she found Miles's lone gaze in a sea of theatre seats. As fate would have it, Della was at the afterparty. Right after Miles had cornered Yule and had given his business pitch and card, Miles turned to find Della in the most iconic image he's ever seen of a woman. Della stood statuesque in a red dress, with her hands down by her side, a slight tension in her fingers, as if recognizing something about the goddess in the painting that resonates with something inside of herself; all the while, a tunic-wearing harpist played softly in the background.

Beauty aside, Della possesses this intangible thing that puts every other woman into one sole category: not her.

Miles, poised for the swing, checks all his angles and everything seems to line up perfect. He swings softly and the ball travels slowly on up to the lip of the hole and tips in. He sighs with a sense of accomplishment. He doesn't need months or years to decide on a wife. He has no reason to believe that Della is anything other than who she presents herself to be.

Miles looks in the direction of the chateau and finds Pop making his way over, with a sense of urgency, unaware that Dutch is hot on his heels.

Chapter 19
What Della's Not Finna Do

Della hadn't had much time with her thoughts. She didn't spend last night staring at the ceiling contemplating matrimony. Just after lovemaking she had dozed off on Miles's chest. This morning, since Miles had cut out early, Della ended up having breakfast with Madison. They leave the breakfast table with tentative plans for shopping, but for now, Della is on her way to the spa appointment with Sage. She's walking down the hallway, guided by a map on the back of a brochure. By the rhythmic click of her high heeled steps, Della is hypnotized in deep thought.

She thinks about the future. She thinks about the conversation she'd had over breakfast with Madison who talked nonstop about trivial things. It's as if Madison's maturation was stunted by wealth, or maybe Della's maturation was accelerated by the lack of it, for the personal sacrifices and the daily negotiation of need and want. Being that Madison is on age with Della, it helps Della believe she's more ready to be a wife than her number of years would indicate. Ready or not, it's happening. It's happening too fast for comfort, but Della isn't about to be that girl who says no to an attractive billionaire out of fear.

Fear, however, was once Della's toxic trait. More specifically, anxiety. It made her introverted as a child, yet as a dancer, it became the key to her success because it scares her into overpreparation.

With love, anxiety makes Della suspect of her feelings for Miles, even though she's well aware that there's no man past, present, nor no man Della can fathom in the future that could make her feel the way Miles makes her feel. Her feelings, however, are so strong, so soon, Della wonders if it's the sex. She wonders when the rose-colored glasses of this new relationship comes down, what will she see? Other than that, Della really can't conjure any reason to give her pause – until she enters the spa and pauses at the sight of Sage at the desk, cursing the clerk in Patois. Della could only decipher one phrase, when Sage points finger and tells the clerk, "…Suck ya mudda front!"

To this scene, Della's internal voice of anxiety narrates, *There's our reason to worry. Miles was reared by* this *woman.* Della suddenly realizes that she will never know the real Miles until the damage from his abusive mother surfaces. "Sage," Della calls softly.

"Hey," Sage says, looking her up and down. "After ya stormed off last night, I didn't think you'd show up."

Had Della known she wasn't expected she surely would not have come. "Well… I um…"

Sage snaps at the desk clerk. "Galang and get di robes!" Sage's eyes roll north, and she sighs, "Gimme di strent."

Looking to lighten the mood, Della smiles and says, "So, we're speaking Patois today?"

"Only whenna cuss ya off," says Sage. Her eyes narrow thin. "You speak?"

"They've been teaching me at RyRy's Kitchen in Jamaica, Queens. Their jerk shrimp is to die for."

Sage hands Della a robe so soft it feels cut from a cloud.

They enter a pristine spa area. Angelic music plays. There's silver trays of champagne and hors d'oeuvres.

They lie down on twin tables for the salt scrub. When the therapists set the timers then leave Sage and Della in lounge chairs to allow the purifying wrap to do its work, the real conversation begins.

Sage initiates. "I know a little something about ballet. I know that in order to make it at the professional level, you had to have been doing it consistently nearly all your life; you can't just show up one day and put on the shoes."

"Very true," Della agrees.

Sage reaches over and touches Della's hand. "Just like being a billionaire's wife. Women who were born into generations of wealth… they just know. This lifestyle is anything but romantic. Your husband will always have a slew of things that come before you. So, if you come into it thinking it's going to be all about you, you're headed for a rude awakening."

Della says, "I'd expect to grow into it like you did. Wait… Or, *were* you groomed for this?"

"Vicariously through my sister. She was high yellow, and my parents believed in the old way; they wanted to ensure that she would marry well, so she could look after the other siblings in the event that something happen to our parents. They made me do all the chores; they didn't want Vivian's hands to harden from dishes and laundry…"

Della's heart breaks for Sage. Not only was she the stuttering child and treated like a bad seed, as Miles had said, but she had to grow up living like a child in a sweatshop and watch her sister be treated like a princess.

"My folks made her the pageant girl, put her in private school and then etiquette school. I made it a point to always help her with those things because it helped me learn for myself."

"Looks like it worked," says Della.

"Vivian married young – to an older man. A bigtime lawyer. She's now widowed and won't marry again for all the world, and I understand why."

Della looks over. "Seriously?"

"More than once, I nearly divorced Mick." Sage says that only their first year of marriage was everything she dreamed it would be, but then Mick returned to reality, a reality where he worked around the clock. Mick is a leader of men first, and a husband second; he got more fulfillment from work than from loving on his wife and that was Sage's first tough pill to swallow. Many evenings Sage spent alone in their mansion, wearing her furs and pearls, awaiting Mick's return, while the sun lowers and the shadows stretch into the living room.

Turns out, Mick was doing more than working; he was partying too, billionaire style. Mick had homes that Sage had no knowledge of. He had a three-hundred-foot yacht docked on the shore of Lake Michigan that Sage had never stepped foot aboard, nor much seen until it was on the news because a woman had overdosed at a party while an Illinois senator was aboard the vessel.

Sage looks at Della, long and hard. "Think you can turn a blind eye to an affair?"

"Pop? An affair?" Della's stiffens. "I can't see it."

"I asked you a question," says Sage.

Della pauses for a moment and answers, "Maybe when you tell me why you did, I might feel differently."

"That's a good answer," replies Sage. Her eyes gaze off into the distance. "Mick and I got married just six months after meeting. When it comes to marriage, these wealthy, powerful men all think alike. They don't need to know you, per se. They need to know that your presence conveys his worth, in the eyes of other men of status. He also needs to know that you're not the type to take the money and run. They want to know you're the type who'd stay despite his indiscretions. They can smell loyalty like a shark to blood." Della wonders if that's why Miles is thinking marriage already.

The more Sage divulges, the more Della's anxiety grows, until she can feel it on her face, like clown paint – to think that, in less time than it takes to prepare for a ballet performance, that she and Miles call themselves prepared to make a lifelong vow before God?

Sage is still going down the litany of offenses she's had to bear, when Della interrupts. "I know why you stayed."

Sage is enraged at the interruption. "I beg your pardon?"

Without even looking at Sage, Della just speaks. "Your entire sense of self-worth is stored in this marriage and this family. I say this respectfully, Sage – that maybe if you had something outside of Pop to really ground you, you would not have endured that. You've normalized it for so long, Sage, that you've come to think it's proper to even ask such a question, as if the ability to tolerate an affair is a prerequisite? But to answer your question, Can I turn a blind eye? Absolutely not. If Miles tried it, I would leave him before he could zip his pants up. Because, for me, walking away from Miles wouldn't mean walking away from everything that gives me purpose."

Sage doesn't interrupt, but she's a stalking predator, ready to leap for the jugular, but by the time Della was done speaking, Sages anger seems to be giving way to curiosity, as if wondering how she'd lost her taste for blood. She reclines back on the lounge chair and gathers her hands over her wrapped belly. Quite matter-of-factly, Sage adds. "My heart is with Haiti. Advancing their causes is something I've always wanted to do. I have the power to, but have not. This deal could be the beginning of me taking on some sort of official role, in tandem with my daughter Corine. I really want this, but it means I'd have to spend a lot of time in the islands. That's just not possible with Mick still running the company."

Della lifts up and aims her wide, determined eyes. "Then Pop should step down."

Sage smiles fondly. "I wish it were that easy. For one, with Brooke now expecting, that pushes everything back. Secondly, everything depends on landing this deal, and honestly, it's not looking good. Whatever they're asking of Mick, it's really testing him, and he seems ready to fold."

Della raises one eyebrow in a nonverbal *And?* "If this deal puts you in position to live out your purpose, Sage, you let Pop know that your heart is on the line and there will be no peace if he doesn't secure this deal and step down… It's *your* time, now. No matter what it takes."

Sage laughs, but stops, because Della isn't. The residue of Sage's laughter hangs in a snide smirk. "Funny how marriage works in the mind of people who have never been married. My time," Sage huffs, and yet something contrary comes over her. Her gaze deepens. The smile melts from her cheeks and lips. Sage echoes, "My time."

Chapter 20
Unorthodox

Dutch's shot rockets up into the sky. Dutch, Pop, and Miles each rear back. Three hands raise, in synchronization, to shade their eyes from the sun. The three cigars Yule gifted them last night, dial up at the exact angle as they locate the golf ball, small in the blue sky, its trajectory banking right. "Damn," says Dutch. The ball falls out of the sky like a shot duck and drops into the sandpit. "Dammit!" Dutch clubs the ground with his driving iron.

Miles says, "I told you to keep your front foot planted."

Dutch's head shakes no. "I told you, I'm unorthodox."

"And *I'm* winning. Pleased to meet you," Miles gloats.

Dutch marches off after the ball.

Pop grabs Miles's wrist to keep him back. "I got something to tell you." Pop pinches his cigar and removes it from his lips. "It's about Della."

Miles's brow flattens. "What could you possibly tell me about my fiancé?"

Just as Pop readies to speak, an oncoming golfcart distracts him. It's Yule. He jumps off of the cart and hits the ground trotting, papers in hand. He asks Miles and Pop to clarify one line item of the proposal and sign another document. As Yule retrieves his pen, he asks, "Have you told him yet?"

Miles says, "Seems he was about to, just before you pulled up." Miles looks at Pop and asks, "So, what is it that you have to tell me, Pop?"

Yule backs out of the tension, saying, "I'll leave you gentlemen to it. See you in a few hours." He hops in the golfcart to return to the meeting with his business partners, but Yule stops. Something catches his eye, but fails to catch his jaw, which drops open. He's in awe of Dutch, who is in the distance, squatting to get a line on his shot. Yule hops off the cart and starts high-stepping towards Dutch. Yule mumbles in French while closing in, his eyes fixed squarely on the bulge of Dutch's backside.

Pop motions to go thwart Yule, but Miles stops him. "Naw Pop. This is about to get interesting," Miles says, with a snarky smile. They take off for a closer look. Yule catches up with Dutch, seemingly to advise him on the correct approach to a bunker shot. Everything about Yule screams pervert, the glean in his eye; how he is so eager, in his insistence, that he pays no mind to his expensive Italian loafers half sunk in pit sand, as he positions himself next to Dutch to demonstrate the proper swing.

Pop and Miles are now close enough to hear. Dutch protests. "I *know*, bro. But what I'm telling you, is that my stance is unorthodox."

"This is basic physics." Yule points a stiff hand at the embankment. "You're shooting out of a bunker. For more lift, lower your grip and put bend in the hips."

Miles is laughing already. Dutch calls, "Miles… Pop… Please come get your boy."

As quick as Dutch voices the request, Yule deftly slides over and hugs Dutch from the rear, supposedly to instruct Dutch on the proper form, but the eagerness in Yules' eyes is that of a humping dog. Dutch spins with a backhand that just misses. "Bitch!"

Yule retreats with palms up. "I was trying to show you."

Miles and Pop hurry to break them up, Miles laughing all the while. Dutch cocks the sand wedge back as if to take a baseball swing and everyone scatters. "I felt his thing on me, man!"

"Chill out Dutch," yells Pop.

"Yes, chilly out," Yule seconds.

Miles again buckles with laughter.

Dutch fires back, "*You* chill out – with that gay shit."

Yule pleads to any who'll listen. "I wasn't being inappropriate, with her."

Dutch fires, "I'm a *him*, you rubber face mother fucker!"

A laughing Miles gathers himself to say, "Give the man the benefit of the doubt."

Dutch with a bulging vein at his neck, fumes, "Ain't no doubt. I told him last night after you got up from the table. I'm a man just like yall."

"But Dutch," says Miles. "You still thick, tho."

Yule approaches, offering a handshake. "I am sorry if you were offended."

"So, you're only sorry if I was offended," Dutch says calmly, but his calm is merely a trap. As soon as Yule gets close enough, Dutch launches a kick that would've struck, if Miles hadn't yanked him back. Dutch yells, "You better stay the fuck away from me dawg, or I'll kick you so hard down there, your nuts'll be lodged in your ass!"

Yule takes off. Miles, Pop, and Dutch are left there coming to grips, and wondering how to return to golfing as usual, after what just took place. Dutch wipes a hand across his face. "Damn near caught me a body, bro," he says as he untucks his shirt and lets it hang to hide his bum.

DELLA sits at one of the chateau's restaurants, at a patio table, trying caviar for the first time. She spits it out in a napkin. To the server who so highly recommended it, Della explains, "It's a texture thing." It's also a mental thing: realizing it's actually the unfertilized eggs of sturgeon fish.

Being surrounded on all sides by patrons of wealth and nobility makes Della feel more out of place than the foreign language they murmur at their tables. There's an olive-colored man (Greek? Syrian?) with a wet combover who is also seated alone; he's been eyeing her quite brazenly. Della suppresses her inclination to smile out of nervousness, fearing he'd take it as an invitation, although Della can't help but wonder what he makes of her, nor how she'll explain herself if he were to approach; hang the kissing hand that bears her engagement ring; say she's here on business with her fiancé, who is heir to the McKinnon oil dynasty? It sounds like a fantasy; it *feels* like a fantasy, having lunch at the foot of a castle with a small daub of caviar on such a large plate. With her fork, Della stirs the caviar to the outskirts of the plate and focuses on the avocado, cantaloupe, and toast.

Miles is late. Since he skipped breakfast with Della, he promised to meet her at the restaurant, said he had plenty of time to finish golfing and still meet her there on time. She begins texting Miles as a way to avoid the eyes of the glancing man. The outside seating has a view of the back nine of the golf course. Della realizes she can see Miles and Pop in the distance, but she can't make out who is who. They're both tall and dark. They're both in plaid pants and Shelby hats, both puffing cigars. They have the same masculine torso-turn when they walk. They're like the same man. This is not a good thing, Della thinks, after hearing Sage describe the old Pop as an entitled, self-serving cheat. Della could never endure as much, while waiting on Miles to learn to respect her properly, as Sage has done for Pop.

A late Miles walks casually across the grass. On his own slow time, he makes his way into the restaurant's main entrance and strolls through the dining area out to the patio. All the while Della is stewing, irritated with the man for being late, but more for him looking like his father.

Miles comes up from behind and says, "You look immaculate, babe."

She denies the kiss with a wrinkled nose. "Didn't know you smoke cigars," she says.

Miles takes the seat across from her. He was going to save the story for later, but laughter is coming over him again. "The craziest thing happened out there," Miles says.

Della's eyes take aim, her mouth fires, "Does this 'thing' explain what kept you so long?"

Miles pauses to study her. "What's up with you?"

"What's up with *you*? You're late. Hanging with the fellas more important than your future wife?"

Miles gasps. "We haven't been engaged one day and already you're drawing lines in the sand?"

"And you're already dismissing my feelings?" Della gets up. "I've lost my appetite." She smooths her dress and snatches up her purse in lazy-eyed annoyance.

Miles says, "I'm not about to beg you to stay."

Della gives one last cut of her eye and walks off.

Although Miles is upset, he bites his lip as he watches Della's walk out, with her valentine shaped calves.

Dutch is on the way in. Della brushes past him without a pardon. In response, Dutch comes to Miles, with the uneven brow that the encounter with Della had produced. "Everything a'ight?"

"It's gone *be* alright," Miles answers.

Dutch sits in Della's vacated seat, shaking his head. "These women, man, I tell ya…"

The server is surprised at two new patrons around Della's abandoned plate of caviar. "Do you need menus?"

Miles wiggles a stiff hand; they place orders for drinks.

Dutch's elbows stand on the table; he then peeks around his clasped hands to say, "Do you know what your sister had the nerve to ask me, bro?"

"What?"

Dutch glances around conspicuously then says, "We're trying to have a kid, right… How Liza gone ask me to carry the baby, bro? *Me!*"

"Damn." Miles tugs his ear and looks away. "How did you respond, though? I only ask because I know my sister. If you give her any inkling that you'd even consider it, it's a wrap. She's gonna apply pressure until you fold."

Dutch sighs and says, "I gotta admit, though, that it makes perfect sense – considering our situation."

Miles raises a halting hand. "Actually, Dutch, this convo is a bit heavy for me right now. I better go check on Della," Miles says. He swipes his drink from the server's delivery tray, gives Dutch a pound, and then heads upstairs.

Dutch can't bear to look across the room at his wife, Eliza, who spies from behind an open menu.

The moment Miles disappears, Eliza hurries over, asking, "What happened?"

Dutch gulps from a frothy mug and then belches. "I was gonna talk to him on the golf course, but then that dude Yule threw things off big time." Dutch raises his guard like a boxer. "Should've seen me in action babe."

Eliza remembers from the text. "I'm less interested in how you handled yourself like a thug, right now." Eliza becomes an image of concern as she bends toward her husband. "You need to be still and meditate on what happened; process your emotions, love. That man sexually assault you. Let's call a spade a spade."

"Me? Sexually assaulted, as if–" Dutch quits with a gasp, and stares at his wife with his fingers rapping the table.

"When I got that text, I almost called the police."

Dutch slaps the table, "Fuck outta here, Liza. This me, baby. I'm from da A–"

"–Aht, aht, people who grew up in Buckhead mansions are from Atlanta, not da A," Liza smarts, with batting lashes. This only amps Dutch even more.

Dutch makes what appears to be gang signs, fingers turned down and dipping in imaginary sauce. "I'm from the bricks, baby. See, you fell in love with the college dude. But back in the hood call me Over-dawg. Fuck is you talmbout'. I break bread with hitters. Street Disciples, six-star. Ask about me," Dutch says with such energy, a boy nearby bobs his head, assuming Dutch was freestyling.

Eliza stares blankly. "I *did* ask about you, and they say you are not hard, Joelle. You always get like this around Miles and Pop, and it's embarrassing."

"Embarrassing, huh… I embarrass you, is that what you're saying?" An awful calm comes over Dutch. He gazes ahead with glassy eyes in the essence of Terrence Howard in every movie he's been in. "What's the matter with you, mane? You're not helping. All you finna do, is cause me get up from this table, go find that Yule and handle him like I should have."

Liza gives a look of hopelessness and changes the subject. "The only thing I want you to handle, is asking Miles to be our donor. *You* insisted that you be the one to ask him and yet you won't ask him."

"Gimme time, sweetheart."

"You had all day yesterday and today."

Dutch takes another swig from the mug and comes away with a froth mustache. "One man can't just pull another man aside and be like…" Dutch switches character, rubbing his chin in cockeyed masculine intensity. "…Yo, lemme get that shperm nigga."

Pop enters the suite with a foot stopping the door while he sets his golf bag inside. He spots Sage who's seated facing the door as if on hold for his return. "How was the spa," asks Pop. Hearing no reply, Pop realizes that Sage had been sitting there sipping wine in her spa robe for who knows how long, stewing about something.

Sage sets the wine down, gets up and strides toward her husband, not a word issued.

"What is this," asks Pop who seems hesitant to enter.

Sage says, "Let the door close behind you, Mick."

In the time it takes the door to swing closed, Sage has walked within arm's reach and set the side of Pop's face on fire with a slap.

His turned head recenters truculently. "Have you lost your got damn *mind*," Pop yells, but the sight of tears racing down Sage's cheek humbles him.

Miserably, she says, "I deserved better." Sage smears a tear with the heel of her hand. Pop attempts to hold Sage, but she stiff-arm's his chest. "The life you've given me, helps me swallow many things. Not betrayal. Not that."

Mick pats his chest. "Did I ever say that it should've? Would I have tried so hard to hide it, or done everything I could to try and make it right?"

"It tore me up, Mick. It changed my heart forever."

The word forever seems to shove Pop off a ledge. Emotionally, he's plummeting backwards down an abys, eyes stretched with terror. "Forever, Sage?"

"And yet I gave you love I no longer had. Because my revenge was to never waiver, so that it would deepen your feelings of guilt."

"Wait a minute, Sage," Mick pleads. "Just wait a second, okay… We were good, just this morning at breakfast. What happened between then and now?"

The hands wiping Sage's face comes down as fists; the very tears of past pain tight in her grasp. "You've dictated everything in this marriage–"

"–But for you!"

"Then it should be no problem, you doing what I'm about to ask you to do, *for me.*"

Pop turns, showing the side of an eye.

"Step down," Sage fires. "You have capable children to run the company. Brooke… Miles… I've always been the wife to stand by you. Now you stand by me. It's *my* time."

"And if I don't step down?"

"It proves we never had a true marriage to begin with."

Pop pinches his nose bridge as if to stop a bleed. "So… divorce, for real this time?"

Sage winces, the mere suggestion as unpalatable as a lemon. "Let's just say that from now on, you'll get the version of me that you deserve."

Pop waits quietly for more, but his wife is done. She turns and heads towards the den to be alone. "Ok," Pop responds. "Alright," he nods, though neither response is an agreement; it's simply an acknowledgement of the terms.

Sage stops and turns in the den. "And if you think about tanking the negotiations as a way to sabotage what I'm trying to doing in Haiti, only then should you start preparing for divorce."

PART V

Chapter 21
The Text

Negotiations go along as expected until Yule, to the dismay of his partners, rescinds his endorsement, citing some vague explanation that leaves everyone scratching their heads, except for Pop, the one person besides Yule that's privy to the real reason. They plan to reconvene in forty-eight hours.

For now, Miles and Pop sit elbow to elbow at the bar, drinking away their sorrow. Pop is also thinking of an angle from which to approach the topic of Della. It's more difficult than Pop had imagined, having to break the heart of the man he once held as an infant in his arms.

Miles sighs. "I should've put more emphasis on the emission targets."

Pop hunches over his glass. "It wasn't the presentation, son. They were lapping it up until Yule, out of nowhere, threw that monkey wrench."

"There's gotta be more to it," Miles says, as his glass comes down. "He's bitter about Dutch, ya think?"

Pop returns a look of ridicule.

"Anyhow," says Miles. "I was off my game. I should've spent all my time finetuning the presentation, instead of arguing with Della."

Pop turns, a look of interest where empathy should be.

"Yup," says Miles. "By the way, the engagement is off."

"The engagement is off," Pop parrots. "You should've told me sooner," says Pop, knowing if he'd been able to relay this information to Yule prior to the negotiations, the deal would've been done, and the dark cloud of Sage divorcing him would've passed on.

"Really, Pop? I could be heartbroken, for all you know, and you're only concerned about being informed sooner?"

Pop shrugs and shows palms cradling his dismay like a baby. "I mean, I do think it's unfortunate…"

Miles's confusion sours more, as if he doesn't recognize his own father. "I see you're not gonna ask what happened… Guess I'll tell you anyway," says Miles. "After we came off the golf course, she was already upset, just sitting there, with an attitude–"

"–You know what." Pop turns. "So was Sage."

"You *know* what took place right before that, right," Miles quizzes. "Della and mom were at the spa. You know mom doesn't want us together, so I think she planted some ideas in Della's head."

Pop's eyes fall closed in light of his private revelation, how Sage, after spending the afternoon with Della – a nontraditional, Gen-Z-er who obviously filled Sage's head with selfish ideas disguised as empowerment. Now Sage is leveraging Pop's indiscretions to shift the balance in their marriage. Pop sighs and says, "Obviously Sage wasn't the only one planting ideas."

Miles, though puzzled by Pop's comment, bypasses it to stay on track. "So Della and I argued for a while. I kept questioning her, trying to get to the root of it… You'll never guess what she ended up telling me."

"What?" Pop waits to be humored.

"She fears I'll become the kind of husband you were."

Pop's face tightens and veers away. "Couldn't wait to drop that one on me, huh, Miles. Got somebody else's words to say what you wanted to say for years now."

Miles observes with slow moving eyes, just to show that he's not rattled. "Ain't nobody talking for me. But that liquor talking for *you* right now. Lemme tell this bartender to gone and cut you off."

Pop ignores his son's humor and presses on. "Bet you even visualized it in advance – how it would play out. It probably never entered the realm of possibility that I'd turn around in my barstool, just like I'm doing now, to enlighten you, that the words of a pill-popping addict doesn't carry much weight with me."

"Wait. What?" Miles pumps brakes with a hand. "Pop. We me may have called off the engagement – taking it slow and what not – but she's still my lady, alright."

"That's where you're wrong, son." Pop leans in like a seasoned informant. "She's Aubrey's lady."

The name ambushes Miles mid-swig and he has a coughing fit, still his head shakes no in advance of his ability to verbally challenge Pop's theory.

Pop, who doesn't so much as pat his coughing son's back, takes the opportunity to tell Miles of everything Yule shared about Della.

In a space between coughs Miles says, "That's laughable." He's coughing again, barking like a yard dog.

Pop just looks at him and shakes his head.

As soon as Miles is able, he indeed laughs at the notion of Della being an addict and giving sex to a physical therapist who pays her in prescriptions.

Pop, with frustration heavy in his brow, says, "If you're in the CEO seat, the mere *allegation* is damaging enough, Miles.

You know that. You may not get ousted for it, but you can't be effective if no one in the boardroom trusts your judgement."

Miles snickers, "But how would they trust the judgement of a CEO who takes hearsay from a pervert?"

The more Pop insists, the more Miles refuses, although internally, with this new information, he begins reimagining what he observed the night he and Della met: Aubrey's jealousy, the pill bottle he cuffed to her. "Whatever Pop. I know Della."

As Miles closes out his tab, he's still smiling in resistance. Pop smiles to disguise his frustration. With so many teeth shown between the two, it's hard to tell that they're arguing. Pop says, "She got your nose wide open and your eyes wide shut." Pop wiggles a finger by his head, adding, "Why does it surprise me? It's happened before."

"Good one, Pop," Miles laughs, while pointing finger pistol. "But that was simply a one-nighter who carried some papers with her, on the way out. I'm more selective about the woman who'll one day carry my child."

"She got you *thinking* that… That dancer-chick isn't fixing to carry a baby further than she can spit."

Miles snickers as he steps out from his stool and leaves.

Pop calls behind him and says, "I almost forgot. Yule said you need to check her text messages ASAP."

Miles is so upset, he's in a deep trance as he enters the suite. Della is on the phone with the limo driver confirming that she and her *boyfriend* Miles are about ready to leave for their dinner reservations in downtown Paris.

Della covers the phone to greet Miles with a kiss, but he doesn't bend; he remains upright, rigid, and out of reach. An honest miscue, Della assumes. Miles slides away and goes into the bathroom, searching for something. He doesn't realize that Della had ended the call and followed him, until he turns to leave. She leans at the entrance, worried, her white dress in stark contrast against her skin, which glistens like brown topaz. "The limo is on the way … wait, is something wrong?"

"It's nothing," Miles replies, but the way he sidesteps her upon exiting the bathroom lets Della know that it's definitely something. "You've been drinking." Della folds her arms. "I can smell it. I thought taking it slow was something we both wanted. And you come in here, you don't kiss me, you just… No wait," she cancels. "Did the deal fall through? That's why you're upset?"

He goes to the den and spins around, scanning. He doubles back to the bedroom without a response, as if Della is a ghost that Miles cannot see nor hear. Della, draped in an all-white, floor-length gown, floats after him.

Miles swipes a pill bottle off the dresser. "What is this?"

"What is what," Della asks, despite Miles holding the pill bottle up by his face like he's its brand ambassador. Della cannot fathom Miles's concern over such a thing.

Miles shakes it like a baby rattle. "This is probably the same bottle Aubrey gave you the night we met, huh?"

"Miles, I know you're not trying to imply," Della says, while pinching the bone between her eyes; the hand drops. "I just *know* you're not…"

Looking at Della, Miles sees the folly in accusing this graceful, sensible, and innocent young woman of being a junkie on the low, but he can't ignore facts, no matter how difficult, even if he has to force the question out like a fake burp. "Are you addicted?"

"Are you a camel? That's how stupid you sound if—" She stops because Miles starts yelling, and in that moment, Della feels as if this is her first time witnessing the influence of his toxic mother.

"…Aubrey H. Jennings M.D.," Miles yells, reciting the name on the medicine bottle loud enough to change the pulse of the discussion. There's no turning back. Miles is now fully committed to going through with this. "I wondered why he was so jealous after walking in on us."

Della backs away as if she'd walked into a gruesome scene. Half looking away, half able to stand the sight of him, she points. "You're serious? You're actually entertaining some mess like this?"

"I had my suspicions, but somehow held you above it."

Della comes forward, finger-jabbing his chest on each word. "As! You! Should!"

"Why? You think just because I'm in love with you, that I should wear a blindfold?"

"Wait," Della says. A hand covers her mouth. Again, she comes towards Miles, but this time, gently. "What did you just say?"

His expression has softened noticeably; he realizes what Della wants him to repeat. "I said, I can't turn a blind eye."

Della's hands rotate in reverse. "No, before that."

Miles rolls his eyes and relents, "I'm in love with you, Della, a'ight. What'd you thought?"

Della beams into his eyes, as if she has never been more certain about anything, or anyone. "What I think, is that we've known each other for only two and a half weeks, Miles, and yet… with no reservations, I'm telling you that I'm in love with you too." Della leans into his chest as if eavesdropping on his heart.

Miles holds Della and says, "I believe you, Della. I felt stupid even questioning you about that."

Della squeezes him. "Let's just stay right here for a moment. This is where we need to be, Miles. We don't need to be fighting."

Miles kisses her forehead and says, "Is it really fighting, if we have makeup sex the same day? For all that mouth, you bout to get punished later on tonight."

He licks his lips and stares her down with such a sexy, carnal drip that Della has to resist promptly crawling onto the bed, where being 'punished' is precisely what she'd look back and beg for, in her best porn voice.

Miles says, "In fact, call back and cancel the limo."

Della looks up, stunned. "Is it that serious?"

Miles winks, "You're about to find out."

Della makes the call and wedges the phone between her face and shoulder while she begins unbuckling Mile's belt.

Miles kisses her neck, while she explains, through the phone, "We won't be going out to dinner again. Looks like we'll be ordering room service–" Miles snatches the phone and tosses it on the bed.

Miles's shirt is open. Della kisses his chest. Miles leans to suck Della's ear lobe but also to get an angle to locate the phone on the bed, ensuring he'd snatched it from Della before she had a chance to lock the screen. Pop had raised enough doubt in Miles that he now must see the text messages, as Yule had recommended. He has maybe twenty seconds before Della's screen locks automatically, so Miles lays her on the bed. He peppers her with kisses, for which Della seems insatiable. All the while, his hand eases over and taps the screen to keep it awake.

Della is purring with anticipation, now that they've professed their love and have broken into a new level in their relationship, which is why she's concerned that Miles, on the other hand, seems quite distracted. Della, wanting nothing less than his full attention and intensity, grabs his face with both hands and asks, "Are you okay, baby?"

Miles now has the answer. Aubrey's final text to Della stops his heart. Miles shows Della the phone screen. "Now why would Aubrey this message, if you're not using?"

Staring Della in the face is one of the many ignored messages that Aubrey sent out of anger; it reads, *I wish you well and I hope you'll one day seek help for your addiction.*

Della snatches her phone, livid. "You lied and said you love me, just to get into my phone!"

"I didn't lie about that," Miles says, as he gets up and retreats. "But I'm not the focus, here. What about that text – sent for your eyes only! Aubrey can lie to other people, but he can't lie to you."

"Oh he can't?" Della swipes through the messages. "Look! He's calling me dizzy bitch, a clout chasing whore, saying I owe him some pussy. Says he thinks me and Natalia 'licky-licky.' You wanna believe that too!" Della is now kneeling upright on the bed. "I was ignoring Aubrey and he was trying say anything to get a response out of me, and the only reason I didn't delete these messages is because I'm gonna use them to get a fucking restraining order when I get back to the states!"

Miles, leaning against the dresser and buttoning his shirt, says, "Can you calm down please?"

"Calm down!" The request backfires. Della springs to her feet, and swipes the pill bottle. "And *your* simple ass, accusing me of getting high with Fenoprofen? This isn't painkillers, dipshit! It's an anti-inflammatory. Google it."

Miles gives a lazy-eyed, "Are you done?"

It's the worst thing you could ever say to Della in an argument; her eyes stretch wide. "Am I *done?*" Della winds the pill bottle back and steps into the throw, releasing on *bitch*, with everything she's got.

Miles catches it like it's nothing, as if his palm is a magnet. Miles counters, "*This* bottle may be legit, but what about all the pills I haven't seen? How many other people have their doctor in their friendzone? That ain't normal."

Della's head lowers and laughs, but it's a laughter of futility, which carries over into weeping. Della touches her temple with a trembling hand. "I would've never imagined me, one day trying to prove to someone that I'm not a dope-fiend. You're a good judge of character, Miles. Does it seem to you like I'm the type of person to be on drugs?"

Miles looks her over with clinical scrutiny. "You got your ways about you."

"I got my ways about me?" Della's face prunes and looks away, ashamed of her tears.

He reaches for her, tenderly. "This doesn't mean that I don't love you, Della. I *do* love you–"

"–If you're breaking up with me right now, you really suck at it, okay. Can you just go? I need to be alone."

Miles only takes in the breath he'd use to explain how he'd lost Pop's faith before, so Pop is not about to hand him the reigns of the multi-billion-dollar family legacy if he doesn't handle this situation responsibly, but before Miles could utter the first word, Della yells, "*Please!* Just go!"

He leaves without a fight. When Miles closes the door behind him, Della backs against it and slides down, sinking in misery.

Della's heart has taken sick; her mind, diseased with cynicism, cursing the thought of ever trying a thing as foolish as love – especially when the result can be as painful and humiliating as this.

Chapter 22
The Proposition

This is the evening of the ball and Della won't be attending. Miles, fully dressed in his tux, is hesitant to leave. Their breakup has wounded her, and Miles feels the responsibility to tend her wounds before tending his own, but that's impossible, as long as Della's pretending she isn't affected all. Just this morning, Della called their failed relationship a fun little experiment – and when Miles referred to them as exes, she gave him a slanted look and replied, "Hardly. It was two weeks, son." This comes just one day after Della had cried a snot bubble the size of a light bulb.

Della, on the other hand, she doesn't buy Miles's nonchalant act. When she sashays across the suite in her mini shirt and cloth booty shorts, she senses his internal conflict. Della does a brisk, hip switching walk over to the coffee table, her passing breeze rich with cocoa butter. Not so obviously, she bends to pick up a hair clip.

Miles gazes and licks his chops like a begging dog. "I know what you're trying to do," he says, bitterly. "Don't make me break out my grey sweatpants," he kids.

Della pivots, alert. "Did you say something?"

On Della's return, she pinches his cheek. "Looking rather dapper, young man." She then sits Indian style on the bed in front of her laptop. After a few beats of silence, aside from the rattle of her typing, Della's head swivels to Miles, her face as plain as a porcelain doll's when she says, "Aren't you running late?"

Miles leaves without a goodbye.

As soon as Miles leaves, Della grabs the Kleenex box she'd hid under the pillow, then pulls the covers over her head, providing a little cave of sorrow in which to weep.

Just outside, Miles has a moment. His jaw and fists tighten as if to fight the door. He then backs away and heads down the hallway, disgusted with himself. Della's obviously trying to both tempt him and piss him off and it's working on both fronts.

When Miles reaches the ballroom, it all looks like a dream. For Miles, it's not the atmosphere, which reeks of wealth, with velvet fabric slung across the ceiling, an elegant champagne fountain the size of an ostrich, and soft speaking butlers who appear as refined as the guests. It's not the Victorian crystal chandelier with fifty lamps, illuminating this angelic aura over a sparsely populated dance floor. It's his mother and father, dancing.

Under the heavenly lighting of the chandelier, Pop and Sage look more intense than Miles has ever seen them. Pop's right hand holds Sage's left hand high; his head leans slightly back while he peers into the eyes of his wife. They've been together for longer than Miles's life on earth, and suddenly now their fascination with each other seems quite new. They turn clockwise and waltz counter-clockwise around the dance floor as if ice skating without a care in the world. They are the picture of the future Miles had envisioned with Della.

Miles wonders what has changed; the promise of a new grandchild on the way? No, Miles thinks. It's deeper.

Miles makes his way over to their table, arriving at the same time that Pop holds out Sage's chair.

Miles just stands there eyeing them to elicit a response.

Sage doubletakes. "Where's Della?"

Miles grimaces and shakes his head no. "She's not feeling well." Miles catches a sly look from Pop, letting him know to tread carefully.

Sage says, "That's too bad. I was really looking forward to seeing her."

"Why? So you and Pop can have one more couple to outshine," Miles says, as he touches fists with Pop. "Got the old man out here doing the ballroom Stanky Leg."

Pop and Sage adjust in their seats, eyeing each other as if negotiating who should break the news. Pop obliges. "I'm stepping down – effective immediately." He throws an arm around Sage. "You see me dancing because your mom and I have come to the realization that you only get one life to get it right. For the foreseeable future, we'll be spending half the year in Haiti. Guess who's gonna be the new Vanguard Energy CEO?"

Miles, in the few seconds he has to respond, considers what if it's not him. Despite Brooke refusing to continue if it meant opening the site in North Dakota, Miles considers, what if it *is* Brooke? For Miles, there would be no pressure from a board of investors questioning his judgement because of allegations surrounding who he marries. Miles shrugs and says, "Why I gotta guess, when you can just tell me?" Miles readies himself to run up to their suite to ask Della to marry him all over again as soon as he hears the name of his sister.

"It's you, killa," Pop says.

Miles smiles through the heartbreak.

"In fact," Pop stands. "Let's go celebrate with a drink."

Miles looks at the champagne fountain and says, "You know I don't really do champagne like that."

Pop smirks, "Who's talking about champagne?"

Miles, with a heavy heart, trails behind Pop, who seeks out Yule, who then leads them through the sanctuary and behind the secret wall. Miles slows down with a tentative, "Yo…"

Pop says, "This is the way to Yule's private stock."

Yule adds, "We're about to enter hallowed ground. Over many centuries, only a few have ever seen it."

They enter the heavy door bearing the Montressor's former coat of arms. Miles is spooked by the darkness. Yule takes two of the electric torches, from their wall holsters, hands one to Pop and in a halo of blueish light, they descend the catacombs. Miles asks, "So we're underneath the chateau right now?"

"Yes," answers Yule. Then, remembering Mick's scare, Yule adds, "I guess I should tell you in advance–" Yule is interrupted by a nudge from Pop.

Pop says, "Let's not ruin it."

As they approach the first bend, Pop shines his torch directly at a dense cluster of skulls. Miles doesn't notice right way. As they close in, Pop counts down from three.

Miles, on one, spots a rack of teeth then pivots and marches the other way like a toy soldier. "Nope!"

Pop and Yule cackle like chimps.

"I'm gettin' the hell outta here." Miles disappears in darkness but quickly returns, reporting, "I can't see my hand in front of my face. Gimme a torch dawg."

Pop replies, "This is how the man does business, Miles. You're the Chief Executive Officer, as of fifteen minutes ago. I guess this is your first test."

Miles sucks it up and moves on. Yule says, to Miles, "Old Geoffrey over there didn't mean to scare you. He welcomes you. *We* welcome you." Yule then leads the way down the corridor.

Miles's head rotates slowly, eerily, to his father, who's using all of his might, not to laugh at this crazy ass Yule who speaks of the dead as if they're still living.

Pop sighs and tugs his suit. "Anyway… Miles? Is Della doing any better than she was yesterday?"

"Night and day. She's taking it *too* well, if you ask me."

Pop counters, "If she's taking it so well, why isn't she attending the ball?"

"Embarrassed… Doesn't wanna face the family after the breakup. She says she's not leaving the suite until it's time to fly home."

In perfect synch, Yule and Pop glance at each other.

Yule says, "We're approaching a nearly three-hundred-year-old barrel of wine – in celebration of you, Miles, taking the helm of the corporation, and the forging of Vanguard's inevitable partnership under the Paris Agreement."

Miles raises a fist in triumph, but then questions it. "But how? We haven't even submitted a counter offer yet."

Again Pop and Yule glance at each other, and this time Miles doesn't let it go. "Are you two keeping secrets?"

Yule answers, "Your father and I have come to an understanding, you see…" Pop gives Yule a searing look that makes Yule change the narrative. "…but really it's my partners; they're quite eager for their… compensation."

The explanation satisfies Miles.

"We are here," announces Yule. He goes to the barrel, unlocks the cylinder, and fills two glasses, for himself and Miles. Yule then reaches toward Pop. "Your glass, Monsieur Mick?"

Pop pats himself down for a moment then curses. "Dammit. I left it upstairs." Pop points with two fingers, split between Yule and Miles. "You two go ahead and start without me."

Miles, for some odd reason, suspects that the mishap was staged, though he couldn't begin to figure out why. He'd suspected some sort of alliance between Yule and Pop since he was startled by the skull, and the two laughed together like a pair of stooges, as if they've been spending more time together on the sly.

So, Mile's first act as sitting CEO is standing in a hall of dead folk, listening to some fool ass Frenchman with a slippery accent tell the story of Fortunato.

Pop, now out of their sight, exits the catacombs on churning feet. He runs down the hallway and back through the secret wall and sanctuary. Pop avoids the ballroom altogether enroute to his quarters. He disappears into his suite empty handed; he exits with a briefcase and a sweat bead at his temple. He takes off, but slowly approaches an intersecting hallway because he hears the voice of his daughter Eliza. He peers around the corner. She's not approaching; Eliza and Dutch are posted on the wall across from the gift shop, arguing in whispers. Pop removes his shoes and snoops past, unseen. Once he's in the clear, he puts his shoes back and heads up to Miles and Della's suite.

Pop knocks again and again. "Della? Della, this is Mick." He begins to wonder if Della is in the suite at all. Wishing it hadn't come to this, Pop takes out the electronic room key that Yule had given him and looks at it. This is something he would never have done if not for Vanguard's situation and if the sake of his marriage were not at stake. He looks up and gives a brief prayer of forgiveness for what he is about to do.

Pop swipes the card key and enters the room like a reluctant burglar, snooping quietly with both hands behind his back. Nervously, Pop calls out, "Are you dressed?"

Della's head pops out, blankets up to her eyes. And this is how Pop sees her. Della holds her scream, figuring it best to get some facts strait. "How'd you get in here? Did you use Miles's key?"

Pop sighs. "We have to talk." He takes his hands from behind his back; one has a briefcase in its grasp.

"Did something happen to Miles? Is he okay?"

"Miles is ok." Pop, feeling like an bona fide creep, continues, "This is very uncomfortable for me, but I had to come talk to you. I feel really bad about how it ended between you and my son."

"You *should* feel bad. You're the one who told him those lies about me." Della tosses the blanket and sits up.

"You've been crying," says Pop.

"That's what happens when you're in love, but you would know anything about that." Della stands, as if ready to go off on this man who is old enough to be her father.

Pop shields his eyes because her mini shirt exposes her whole belly, so flat that it looks missing. "I know how you must feel. One day you're set to marry into one of the wealthiest families in the country and have all the burdens of life lifted away, but now, so suddenly, all of that has vanished," Pop says, while unlocking the briefcase and laying it open on the dresser. "I just hate that you're now walking away with nothing." Pop steps away from the briefcase. "But I have an opportunity for you that can change all that. Just hear me out, will you?"

Della, in all her life, has only seen that amount of cash in movies. She can't even look away from it. Slowly, she grapples the blanket to cover her body. "What is that?"

Pop says, "Let's call it severance pay. I'll give you some instructions, and if you agree, I'll leave this right here."

Della couldn't imagine what she'd have to do, to own that briefcase; smuggle jewels through customs, perhaps? All that cash – that life altering sum of money – forces Della to at least listen to what Pop has to say.

Chapter 23
The Old Switcheroo

Miles checks his watch, wondering what's taking Pop so long. His right ear has gone numb, hearing Yule talk about the greatness of his lineage, when decaying skulls with severe genetic underbites is the only way in which Miles will ever see them. When Yule finally changed subjects, Miles was grateful, initially, but by now he's grown weary of Yule's next topic; defending his actions on the golf course.

Yule shrugs. "…Was my attempt to instruct Monsieur Dutch clumsy? Yes. But inappropriate? No." To Miles's indifference, Yule concedes at least one thing, "I recently have developed a thing for ethnic women, and… maybe I was a bit excited when I saw that… that rump–"

"–But that rump belongs to a man," Miles counters.

Yule's eyes roll to his guest. "And yet you – mister big cis man – are here with the likes of me, having drinks in the dark?"

He'd punch Yule in the side of the head if the oilfields weren't drying up and if Yule's endorsement wasn't the saving grace for the McKinnon dynasty. Miles settles for a stern warning. "I don't even play like that, bruh."

They pause because they hear footsteps. Pop emerges from the darkness, alert as a fugitive; the torch illuminates a light sweat upon his forehead.

Yule asks, "Is everything alright?"

Pop replies, "Everything is definitely alright, one hundred percent." He then smiles at his son and asks, "What do you think about the wine?"

"Tastes like a raisin and kerosene cocktail, but I'm getting used to it."

"And how many have you had?"

Miles looks to Yule. "We on number what, five, six? I don't feel shit though."

Pop pats Miles's shoulder with a hand of experience. "You will, son. Trust me, you will."

A voice calls from down the corridor. "Ay, Pop! Who all's down here?"

Pop turns to the voice, his profile as stern as an eagle's. "Is that... Hey Dutch! Come straight on back."

"How, Pop? I can't see a got-damn thing."

Pop takes his torch to go retrieve Dutch. On their way back, there is a high-pitched scream, Dutch, obviously startled by the skeletons. A tickled Miles makes the mistake of looking over at Yule who is also holding his laughter. Finding each other's eyes wide as lemurs' sets them off, snorting in suppressed laughter, for picturing how Dutch's scare must've looked, but moreso for how embarrassed the hypermasculine Dutch must be, after letting out such an effeminate scream.

Yule nudges Miles and says, "Must've scared the eight-year-old girl out of him."

Dutch emerges, holding a champagne glass now spilled empty during the scare. Dutch searches for remnants of laughter on the faces of Miles and Yule, while he asks, "Y'all heard that?"

Miles plays clueless. "Heard what?"

Yule follows his lead, his accent thickened by stress. "Vy, I did not hear a s'ing."

Dutch greets Miles with a fist bump, but that same fist ejects a finger, pointing at Yule. "Y'all keep that fool away from me, yo."

Pop asks, "How did you find this?"

"I followed you, Pop. You came through looking stressed. I thought you was in trouble. And then when I saw you come through the door, I looked in and saw this… I thought this was on some underground bunker type shit – figured maybe you'd discovered that this perv (Yule) had girls trapped down here or somethin'. You know how them pale folk do."

"Be nice, Dutch," says Pop who drops a hand on Yule's shoulder. "This man is our business partner."

Yule touches his palm to his forehead, in distress. "Oh my! Gentlemen, I do believe I've forgotten to personally deliver a wine bottle to the Duke of Estonia. Pardon me." Yule brushes by Pop, who slips him Della's room key.

As soon as the glow from Yule's torch disappears in darkness Miles turns to Dutch. "You got no chill, man."

"What you talkin' about?"

"We already know you tough, Dutch. You don't have to try to prove it every chance you get."

"Whatever man," says Dutch. "What y'all drinkin' on?"

Pop nods at Dutch's empty glass. "Lemme see that."

Pop goes to the barrel and fills the glass. He and Miles eye each other in suspense of Dutch's reaction. Dutch does more than sip; he turns the glass up and chugs, but comes down hissing, two fingers pressed to his throat. "What in the gorilla piss…!" Dutch is flanked with laughter.

Pop warns, "Better go easy. It'll sneak up on ya."

"I'm tellin' ya," Miles seconds, with woozy eyes. "It's coming over me right now as we speak."

"Gimme a refill Pop," says Dutch. "Got me down here in the belly of a graveyard... Y'all don't feel weird? Our three black asses, surrounded by the remains of our colonizers?" Dutch balls up his fists and feints at the skulls on the wall. "Sumbitches."

Miles tries to make a call to Della but realizes there's no signal underground. "Yo Pop, you got a signal?"

Pop replies, "I seem to have lost my phone."

Dutch holds up his phone. "No signal for me either."

Miles and Pop quietly fill their glasses, and in this silence, Dutch realizes his opportunity. "Yo Miles. "Lemme holler at you for a second, bro."

"What's up?"

"I been trying to talk to you alone the whole time we been here in France... Pop's here, but I guess this is the most alone we gone get." Dutch's hand cups over his mouth and smooths down, as if there's a goatee there to stroke. "As I said before, Eliza and me want a kid, right."

Miles's brow raises. "Hold up. Wait. How is this something you need to talk to *me* about."

Pop draws stiff, not even blinking.

Dutch rubs his hands together. "Just hear me out bro."

Pop downs a shot and watches.

Dutch explains in quite thuglike manner, with averting eyes and punching syllables on his palm. "Now, when it comes to the situation with Eliza and me, we not doing no sperm bank nor use some colleague for a donor, nah-mean? I want my seed to be mines. Since there ain't no men left in my immediate family, the only way my seed can be mines is if I carry it, as a man – but doesn't Eliza have the right to pass on her genes as well?" Dutch looks left. "Hey, Pop..." The man flinches. Dutch says, "Don't you want your grandchild to have McKinnon blood in its veins?"

This topic, this spotlight, has Pop so nervous, he tucks his chin and mumbles. "Well, ya see there, Dutch. I just… doggone, ya know…"

"Relax, Pop," says Dutch. "Nobody's asking you, old timer. Damn sperm count probably low enough to 'drop' in a game of Tonk." Dutch turns to the right. "So, what I'm sayin' bruh-law is—"

"—Dutch stop. Don't even let the words leave your lips." Miles points and wobbles, as if that three-hundred-year-old Amontillado has finally snuck up on him. "I can't even bear the question, much less the thing itself." Miles's expression resembles a mugshot pose, showing neither regret for the crime, nor for getting caught. He points two thumbs over in the direction of the exit. "I gotta go check on Della."

"No wait." Pop hurries to block Miles's path, knowing if Miles were to go up to his suite, it would ruin Pop's plan for Yule, who should be entering Della's suite at this very moment. "Miles, listen to what Dutch has to say," Pop pleads. "This is for your sister. Eliza has as much of a right to an heir as you do." Miles still tries to get around his father but Pop grips his upper arms. "Look around you, Miles. Look at these skulls. See those jacked-up teeth survived through the ages? Why? Because they did whatever it took to keep their bloodline." Pop sounds silly even to himself, but it's his only play to keep Miles from returning to his suite. Pop adds, "Do you think that was always easy? Huh? Don't you think somewhere down the line they had infertile male heirs, baron wives — the family decimated by pestilence. You don't think there were times where kin had to lay with kin to produce an heir? What's so taboo about your situation, when Dutch isn't your kin?"

Miles, now visibly drunk, wobbles where he stands. He points to the wall of bones, "With *them*, it was man and woman — not man on man!"

"This is the twenty-first century, Miles. It's just you and a Petrie dish. You don't have to screw Dutch–"

"–Actually, Pop," Dutch interjects, a hand up like a pupil. "You know Eliza," he grins. "Vegan, wholistic, spiritual, so she doesn't want any intervention from modern medicine so, yeah… Miles, I'm telling you, man to man, that uh… you would have to mount me – if you will… But I swear if you kiss me, I'll knock ya teef out."

"Mount you!? *Hell* naw!" Miles breaks away from Pop.

"Miles!" Pop notices Dutch going after Miles, but Pop holds him back with a forearm bar. "Wait." Pop touches a finger to his lips, his eyes lurking, as if listening.

On queue they hear Miles calling back, his words slurring, "Yo! I can't see shit!"

Pop whispers. "He got no choice but to come back."

A stubborn, albeit drunken Miles keeps forward, balancing himself against the wall. After a while, Pop and Dutch hear Miles yelling. "That bastard Yule locked the door on us! We trapped! We trapped down here, man!"

Pop picks up his torch. He and Dutch run to catch up to Miles, all the while hearing a loud thudding sound again and again. They clear the last bend and see Miles lunging shoulder first into the door, but he's too drunk to be effective.

Miles points to a separation in the door frame. "See, it's not locked. Something's propped up behind it."

They check their phones; still no signal. They pace fretfully in front of the entrance. They take turns cursing Yule, and besting each other's promises of how badly they'll beat the brakes off of Yule, on sight.

Dutch goes quiet for a while. Dutch paces like a newly caged wolf who, until now, has only known the boundary of its own territorial scent marks. "Y'all watch out," Dutch says, still pacing, letting his rage build. "I can't stand being closed in. My nanna used to lock me in the closet. I can't stand this shit!

No more... No more..." That little misunderstood Tomboy now cowers behind Dutch who has grown into the person capable of protecting him. Dutch roars and takes off full speed, charging through the door, breaking the wooden chair wedged behind it, but Dutch's momentum carries him stumbling forward into a faceplant.

Miles laughs. "See Dutch, you be doing too much."

Dutch hops up. "Oh shit. Pop?" Dutch pats his nose and checks the palm for blood. "Is there a mark?"

The skin is scraped from the tip of Dutch's nose, and Pop doesn't have the heart to say.

"Man, Dutch your nose pink as a bitch," Miles heckles, but instant karma kicks him in the gut, leaving him bent over, vomit gushing like a spigot.

Chapter 24
The Sting

Della answers before the third knock. Quickly, she backs away deep into the suite, out of arms reach. "Close the door behind you."

Yule's eyes stretch to ensure they're not closed over a dream of being alone with Della in a purple contour dress.

Coldly Della says, "You win – if that's what you need to hear. But no amount of money can make me pretend to enjoy this."

"Money? What money do you speak of? I received a handwritten note requesting my presence here. The note did not say why, but I now see that your attire leaves no room for interpretation."

"Well, did the note also mention anything about you covering the difference? I counted the money and it falls short of the amount I agreed to."

Yules comes further in, his head on a swivel. He huffs, "Your every word is about money?"

"Nothing will transpire without it." Della's steps aside to make way for Yule who goes into the den and then doubles back to look in the bathroom.

Now satisfied that the suite is empty, Yule says, "You make this feel like some sort of entrapment."

"How so?"

"This talk of money. You won't look at me; you won't touch me."

"Honestly, I find you disgusting. Plus you sexually assaulted me before. How many other dancers, Yule?"

"Your questions are quite interesting. Where's your phone? Give it to me."

"You think you're being recorded? Is that why you're acting so weird?" Della points with a toss of her head. "Phone's over there on the dresser."

Yule retrieves it and brings it to Della to unlock the device; he's like an antsy child awaiting a candy wrapper to be opened for him.

Della hands the phone over unlocked. "See? No recording app running – nothing shady. All I want is my money, and *then* you can have what you want."

"What is the deficit?"

"Five hundred dollars."

"Five hundred dollars! I've left bar tips over five hundred dollars."

"Then stop bitching and write me a check."

"Check!" Yule wags a finger. "No paper trail." Yule digs in his wallet. "I have euro. You can exchange it at the bank when you get back to the states." As Yule presses the wad of cash into Della's grasp, he takes the opportunity to grasp her. The grip is more than aggressive; it's vengeful.

"Hey, Yule, easy will ya?" Della tries to pull away, but he yanks her into his body, his breath briny with wine.

"You have your money. What I do *not* have is time."

Della sasses, "You think you've caught me? The only thing you caught yourself is a case. You're being recorded."

"Nice try!"

Della gives it all her strength to wring loose, then backs away and attempts to reason with her attacker. "Wait," says Della. "I'm telling you, there's another phone in here. It's Pop's phone. It's on. And it's recording," Della says, while doubting she's even getting through to Yule because something evil and ghoulish has come over him. The sockets of his eyes darkens, the laugh lines deepen, and his mouth juts in a bulldoggish underbite. He stalks forward at the same rate that Della steps back. Della's back hits the dresser. Her hand reaches behind her, feeling for something on the dresser to clock him with.

"I'm going to enjoy this, you nègre de bas étage!"

Della gives a side-eye. "Wait, did you just call me a nigger in French?" The hand reaching back wraps around what feels like a can of afro sheen.

MILES IS able to channel his focus in order to walk, on his own power, across the ballroom without being an embarrassment. As soon as they exit the far side of the ballroom, Miles stumbles into Pop, who shoulders Miles in the direction of the suite. "C'mon Miles. Hurry, son."

Miles stumbles along, an arm draped over Pop's shoulder like a prize fighter explaining how the opponent got the better of him. "I only had like seven shots, Pop."

"Suck it up, Miles," says Pop. "Yule must've put the chair behind the door because he's trying to hurt Della."

Miles perks up. "Where's Della?"

"In her suite." Miles relaxes for a fraction of a second until Pop adds, "With Yule!"

Miles takes off, shedding his drunkenness like a bathrobe; a sober Pop takes off after him, but pulls up lame, holding a hamstring. Miles is a world class sprinter competing in a tux. He scales the steps three per stride. He reaches the suite in a sliding stop on slick dress shoes. Miles hears a scream. He fumbles with the card. "Della!" His voice echoes down the hallway.

Pop is at the bottom of the stairs bracing on the handrail, yelling, "What's happening up there?"

When Miles's room key swipes and he bursts through, Della is leaping over the bed like an impala, Yule diving at her legs but hugging nothing but air. As Yule flops across the bed on his belly, Miles has him by the collar, yanking him back up. Yule, now realizing how he'd levitated to his feet, screams at the sight of Miles – screams at the drawn black fist springing to the foreground, blotting out the lights as Miles hits Yule's off-switch. Yule goes limp and crumbles by the side of the bed.

Miles and Della run to each other and embrace. Miles has many questions for Pop, and Della, for that matter, but more importantly he asks, "Are you okay?"

"What took you so long," Della yells. "And where the hell is Simms?"

Miles replies, "I'll call him now."

Della's adrenaline is rushing out of her and in comes the nightmare of what nearly happened here, filling her body. Della hugs herself and her eyes and mouth shut tight.

Miles assumed he'd arrived in the nick of time, but watching Della's meltdown now makes him wonder if he was late. "Naw, hell naw, Della don't tell me he… Did he…" Miles asks, needing the answer to decide whether to go over and stomp Yule into a puddle.

Della opens her eyes to answer him, but what she sees is Yule standing behind him with a vase coming down. Miles sees Della's eyes spring open in fear, then he hears a hollow plunk, and the scene blurs away. A screaming Della tries to catch Miles, but ends up smothered by him on the floor. Yule tries to escape in a dash for the door, but he's surprised by Pop and Simms. Pop sees Miles down, Della now crouched and over him and crying. Pop thinks the worst. "What'd you do to my son!" Pop reaches for Simms hip, unholsters his sidearm and aims for Yule's head. Yule's hands clasp in prayer. "Monsieur! Please!"

Della, seeing the gun, screams, "Miles is okay!"

Lucky for Yule the gun's safety is on.

Simms takes the gun from Pop and closes the door behind them. Della stands. "He's ok. He's just out."

Yule starts claiming self-defense. Pop pushes Yule aside, limps over to the wall and removes a painting. Pop's phone was never lost. He'd taped it to the back of the painting, in which he made a hole over the phone's camera.

Yule realizes that Della wasn't lying about being recorded. Yule slaps his forehead and says, "Aye, yai, yai."

Pop begins playing the video back.

Yule sits on the edge of the bed, biting his nails while coming to grips with the realization that life, as he knows it, is now coming to an abrupt end.

Pop forces the phone screen in Yule's face, displaying the moment he attacks Della. "You call this self-defense?"

Yule argues, "If you use this against me, I will see to it that you never do business in all of Europe."

Pop says, "How's that? When this video will guarantee that I do. If you do not comply with all of my demands, you will rot in a jail cell and your bones will sit down there in the catacombs where future generations will point to your skull as the fuckup who set the family back."

Yule, who's eye is now purple and swollen from Miles's punch, weeps in his hands. Pop goes over to help Simms and Della move Miles to the bed. Simms says, "He's out real good. Was he drinking?"

"Heavily," says Pop. "Should we call an ambulance?"

Simms squints and sighs, "They'll have questions. Questions you'd rather not answer. The best thing to do, right now, is let Miles sleep."

Pop demands that the one million dollars that Yule's business partners require, be fronted by Yule himself, and that Yule adds his endorsement to the contract, which will all but solidify Vanguard Energy's partnership under the Paris Agreement.

Yules says, "But what about Della? We have to get her under some sort of nondisclosure. I understand that you paid her, but that doesn't—"

"—I refused the money." Della comes around to face Yule. "All I need is two things from you. The first is to clear my name."

Yule's confusion wrinkles his brow. "Your name? Your name isn't known beyond a few blocks of your address."

"Miles needs to know the truth. So does Pop."

"Pop?" Yule blinks rapidly, clearing his vision in hopes to see the logic in Della using this substantial leverage for such a menial request. "Do I just tell him now?"

"Uh, *yeah*," Della says with hurried nods.

"I lied, Monsieur Mick. Della was never involved with her physical therapist. She actually rejected him. Aubrey was quite bitter, which is why, per my request, he agreed to send a text implying that Della was an addict." Yule looks to Della and says, "Is that it?"

"I said there's two things. The other, is that no other dancer should be subjected to you. You will surrender your position on the board of directors for Manhattan Dance."

Yule grins and runs a hand back over his head. "You can't be serious. If I am not on the board, I can't secure Meredith's position as artistic director. Let *me* pay for my actions, not Meredith." He turns. "Monsieur Mick, this is too much. If I must comply with her demands, as well… I ask that you make a few concessions on your end."

"No concessions on my end," says Pop. Della smiles at Yule, but her smile goes limp when she hears Pop add, "Besides, Yule, you don't have to do anything she says." Della's head swivels to Pop, who continues, "The video is on *my* phone. She doesn't have anything but her word against yours — and mine, as a witness that nothing happened here."

Della's arms drop to her side in disbelief. "You're really gonna do me like this, Pop! After what I just went through!"

"You should've took the money." Pop helps Yule up from the bed. "Go get that contract signed. I'll catch up."

With no hesitation, Yule leaves the room while Pop stays behind to face Della who says, "Pop! You *promised!* I would've *never* went through with this, if I didn't think I could protect the dancers from him in the future."

Pop, who's already leaving, turns his torso to say, "Girl, gone somewhere."

"Really!?" Della comes forward, claws down by her side. "So you're gonna turn this predator loose — let him keep turning innocent young women into victims?"

Pop, with his palms turned up in front of his belly, says, "Don't get me wrong, now, I do feel bad, and I haven't figured out how I'm gonna sleep at night, but I will. You heard Brooke explain our predicament. There's too much at stake. We can't have a deal squeezed on two sides. I've seen it before. It forces you to do business in a way that produces red flags. And we can't risk that, with the level of oversight that comes with a venture like this."

"You were the one feeding Miles all those lies. We would still be together if it wasn't for you."

"You expect an apology from me? When you ran to Yule and told him that Miles had information stolen? What were you thinking?"

"What? I didn't tell Yule anything like that!"

"How else would he know? Miles didn't tell him. *I* sure as hell didn't tell him." Pop gives her a moment's glare then leaves.

Simms, trailing behind him, is the only one there to catch the tail end of Della's plea. "I swear to God I didn't tell Yule anything!"

Simms catches the door the second before it closes behind him. He peeks back in. "Question. If you didn't tell Yule, did you tell anyone at all?"

"No," says Della. "That conversation only came up once, and Miles and I were alone."

"Alone where? In here?"

Della nods.

Simms peeks out of the door and calls out to Pop, promising to catch up soon. Simms then comes into the room, all of his years of experience gathered in his brow.

Simms searches under lampshades, behind pictures and the underside of dresser drawers. He stops to ask, "Where, exactly, did this conversation take place?"

Della is crushed because she knows what he's searching for, and that it's the only logical answer to Yule knowing that information. The question of what else has Yule heard or even seen, sickens her. Della's hands wipe down her face to uncover her mouth. "We were in the bathroom."

Simms goes straight to the bathroom mirror. He puts his nose to the glass. He stares for a moment then backs away. "Two-way mirror." He takes something from his back pocket which unfolds into a knife, which he uses to pry the mirror. Behind it, there's a recession in the wall with a camcorder on a tripod.

"My God," says Della. "*See*, I never told Yule this family's business. He only knew because he was spying."

"The adjoining room is likely unoccupied." Simms grabs the camera and studies it. "Motion detection is on." He opens the back of the camcorder and closes it. "There's a memory card in here. All the footage is stored. I'll let you do the honors," he says, and passes it to Della.

Della takes the camera into the bedroom and sits on the edge of the bed next to a hard-sleeping Miles. She watches the small preview screen and sees herself getting undressed and stepping into the bath; she's never felt so deeply violated. She lowers the device to wipe her tears. "This creep has been watching me?"

Simms goes into the bathroom again, saying, "If anyone asks, you uncovered this yourself." He refastens the mirror then returns to Della who's sitting in the same position he'd left her in. On his way out, Simms sets a hand on Della's shoulder, and says, "You now have leverage again."

Della tries, time and time again, to wake Miles but he can only open his eyes for a few seconds at a time, and even then, he's incoherent. What good would telling him the truth do now anyway, Della thinks. She'd already told Miles her truth and he didn't believe her. She could explain everything that transpired while he was out, and he still won't believe her without Pop to corroborate the events.

She's not looking to tell him the truth in order to save their relationship; she wants him to know what he'd lost – not an addict, but a woman who is everything he believed her to be.

Della takes a deep breath and it's just air filling and deflating her like a bag; she feels desolate inside. Within the hour, she's been betrayed by her fiancé, had learned that her privacy, her intimate moments, was compromised, and she has been assaulted because of an arrangement orchestrated by Pop and Miles – like father like son.

She thinks back to when she was staring at the open briefcase, refusing to go through with Pop's plan, even threatening to tell Miles. Her phone was out, her thumb hovering over Miles's contact like detonator. Pop (knowing Miles had no signal down in the catacombs) encouraged her, *Call him, he'll tell you he's in on it. I'll wait.* Della dialed four times in a row and the call kept going straight to voicemail. Della was in tears, unraveling, and willing to call as many times as she needed to hear Miles's voice, but then Pop placed the weight of his hand on top of Della's, lowering her phone, saying, *Miles probably turned his phone off because he can't face you. He does have feelings for you; I know this, but feelings, for a mere woman, will never come ahead of family.* Pop had then input Simms number in Della's phone on speed-dial, telling her to call the moment she didn't feel safe.

Della had agreed, only because she believed Miles was in on it, which, in effect, cancelled any possible future with him, a man whose one job was to protect her from Yule and yet he helps orchestrate a lick that put her alone in a room with him.

Tears drain down Della's face; she makes no effort to wipe them, as she studies Miles, fuming at his ability to sleep so soundly during one of the lowest moments of her life. Miles shifts and snorts like a bearded Billy goat. On that note, Della decides to begin the long, arduous task of extinguishing the flame she carries for him.

Chapter 25
She Gone

Miles wakes to a knock at the door and Pop calling from the other side.

"Yeah, yeah," Miles grumbles, as he lumbers over and opens the door.

Before Pop sets a toe inside, he asks, "You alright?"

Miles stretches his eyes and rubs the corners. "You'd think I'd be hung over, but nah. No headache or nothing."

"No?" Pop strolls inside, looking around. After peeping into the den, he points to the bathroom. "She in there?"

Miles goes and tests the doorknob. It's unlocked. He opens it. Not only is Della not there, there's no evidence of her having been in there. "Maybe she's downstairs at breakfast," Miles says, as he begins texting her.

Pop says, "I'm surprised you *don't* have a headache. Yule crowned you pretty good with that vase."

Miles looks up from his phone. The blur of last night begins slowing down in his mind to where he can study the events. "What you mean Yule crowned me? Didn't I knock him the fuck out?"

"You know how the song goes. He fell down, but he got up."

"All I remember is…" Miles pauses with his mouth open, his memory turning the pages of last night's picture book. His eyes settle upon his father and scrunches with anger. "How did you know Yule was in here?"

Pop's head droops with shame. "First let me say that… We got Yule's signature. We did it, son. Our profitability, our legacy… is shored up for generations to come. And with you as CEO, you'll always be remembered as the McKinnon who took us from international to global."

Miles rejects the celebratory spin and stands firm in interrogation mode. "You gone answer my question, Pop?"

Pop leans in, leading with an ear. "What'd you call me?"

"What're you talking about? I called you Pop."

"And don't you forget it. *I'm* the father. You're the son. I don't answer to you."

Miles head shakes. "Yeah, you always pull this 'I'm the father' crap when you know you're wrong."

"If the only thing I could do, to get a signature out of that crazy son of a bitch, was to convince Della to dangle herself in front of him like a carrot to a horse… I did that. And it worked. We got Yule on tape agreeing to exchange money for sex."

"Brooo!" Miles's hands run back through his dreads. "You did what!"

"Obviously, I couldn't do it by myself. Yule doesn't wanna fuck me. Della agreed. She played her part in it."

Miles nearly yanks out ropes of hair when his hands come down. "They fucked!?"

Pop's whole torso tosses side to side as he pouts, "No, man! No! I would never cosign something like that."

The many implications crashes over Miles like waves. "She was in on this? The Della *I* know would never do something like that."

Pop, bashful with guilt, replies, "To her credit, she outright refused and she would not budge."

"But did it anyway? How?"

"She said she'd do it only under one condition: if *you* were ok with it."

Miles's fists thrust down at his sides. "Do I look 'ok with it' to you?!"

"Wait one got damn minute." Pop looks away and back, scratching his head, as if he's lost his keys. "Are you bucking up to me, right now? All puffed up like you're fixin' to do something? Boy, I'll cave your damn chest in."

They're brow to brow in height but Miles looks Pop up and down in a few head flicks, as if the man is short. "That intimidation worked on Miles the boy. This is Miles, the man, here. You put your hands on me, it's gone cost you."

Pop inhales as if fueling himself with the testosterone in the air. "Yeah, that's it," Pop encourages, as if he'd seen this day coming all his life; the lion cub now with a full mane, vying for the pride. "I ain't old yet, boy. I fucking dare you."

Miles bites down. "Don't think I won't do it."

Pop revs like a race engine. "*Do* it Miles. *Do* it!"

Miles squares his shoulders for a final word. "You, the father of four daughters, used your money and power, to exploit a young black woman… And because of that…" Miles rolls up his sleeves and says, "…I'm gone tell momma." Miles turns and goes.

Pop high-steps after him. "Hey wait!" He's already in hot water with Sage. Pop catches up to Miles and throws an arm around him to steer him back. "C'mon now, son. No need to involve Sage," says Pop, whose giggle runs like a series of hiccups, the elder lion now yipping like a hyena. "I was just playing, my boy. We can talk it out like men."

"Yeah, that's what I thought." Miles says as he shrugs Pops arm off of his shoulder. Miles fishes his phone from his pocket and checks the screen. "Still no reply." Miles looks around and notices that, oddly, the dresser is clear of Della's makeup and hair supplies. He opens the closet; only his garments hang. "She gone."

"Gone?"

"All her stuff… It's missing." Miles wanders around searching for evidence, knowing the effort is merely exercise, while he continues the conversation. "Since you now wanna talk like men, tell me how you would you feel if someone did, what you did, to one of your daughters?"

"My daughters, their children's children, and so on, is precisely why I did what I did. McKinnons, born long after I'm dead, will always have enough resources and money, to never have to agree to something they'd rather not do."

Miles's brow tweaks. "You pay her? How much?"

"I brought a briefcase of fifty-thousand-dollars. She refused it, actually. That's why I'm here. I feel bad about her going through all this and coming away with nothing."

"She ain't come away with nothing." Miles parts the curtains to see the morning. "She definitely got something. The engagement ring: I told her she could sell it."

Pop is visibly relieved. "So, *that's* why she turned down the money – didn't even need it." He stares at the floor and says, "I mean, she really had me fooled – talkin' about, all she wanted to do was to clear her name."

"Clear her name of what?"

"Oh yeah," Pop raises a number one. "Yule confessed. Della was never involved with the doctor. Also, Yule had him send that text to make you think she was an addict."

"Damn," Miles agonizes. "Damn, damn, damn, man," Miles says, as he opens a drawer and stops at the sight of something – something that makes him stare and chuckle.

Pop smiles readily. "What is it?"

Miles plucks, out of the yawning drawer, the diamond engagement ring that Della left behind. Miles laughs in a peculiar way; he jostles from deep within, as if it's hardly laughter at all, but rather an alternative to crying. Now with Della gone, he has learned that she is, in fact, everything he had believed her to be. His head shakes. "She gone, Pop."

"She's not gone, Miles, *think*. To get an international flight across the Atlantic, last minute? She can't afford that." Pop pats Miles on the back. "For now, just let her have whatever space she needs. She's gotta come back to fly home."

THE TABLES have turned. Sitting opposite of Della is Meredith, Manhattan Dance Company's artistic director who once held the stick as Della's interviewer, when the company lost their lone black ballerina and needed another – at a time when Della, as talented as she is, was a struggling, on-call dancer, wishing injury upon full time dancers just to get a slot. It was at a time when Della wondered if she should focus, instead, on her retail job and work her way up the ranks. Della had credited Meredith with solidifying her career, bringing her on with a prestigious dance company. Della later credited Meredith with lowballing her salary, after Della stumbled upon a payroll report and learned that she was the lowest paid fulltime dancer in the studio, being compensated just a notch above dancers at the apprentice level.

Della now holds the stick via the scathing camcorder video containing footage of Meredith's husband spying; soliciting, and chasing Della in a full-on assault.

They sit opposite of each other, under a glass skylight in the cathedral style living room of Yule and Meredith's two-hundred-year-old mansion, once occupied by the famous French playwright Georges Feydeau. Meredith wears a striped blouse and white capris, her back-length hair bound and draped over a shoulder. Della suspects that the cup of tea, on the end table next to Meredith, is spiked.

Meredith watches the camcorder's mini screen so matter-of-factly, it prompts Della to ask, "This isn't the first time, is it?"

Meredith looks up and stares, as if Della is some intricately patterned wallpaper.

Della leans in. "Is it?"

Meredith has yet to blink. "I'm gonna need both copies of the video."

"I've gotta protect the girls. I keep one copy to ensure that you keep Yule out of the production area, and that he recuses himself from the board of directors."

"No can do. He's my umbrella," says Meredith. "What if, in Yule's absence, they replace me? I can live without Yule; I can *not* live without ballet."

"No one can take ballet from you."

"I will not be satisfied teaching some dance class out of an office rental. I'm a major influence, in the mainstream of per-forming arts. That's where I'll be for as long as I have my wits about me."

"But there *is* a way to keep your position."

"How do you suppose?" Meredith picks up her tea cup, ready to sip and listen.

Della, in all earnestness says, "Earn it. Commit yourself to excellence every day..." Della stops at the tink of the tea cup setting back in its saucer.

Meredith's thin, red painted lips shapes every syllable. "Don't give me that load of crap."

Della, now, is so triggered, she's antsy in her chair. Five fin-gertips draw to a point, as if pinching the offense by the tail. "You call it crap – the idea of you actually earning your keep? Are you actually irritated because I'm not suggesting some point of leverage, or some loophole for you to exploit?" Della crosses her legs and leans back in her chair for a better look at the piece of work before her. A new revelation overrides the first. "Why does this not surprise me? Excellence means nothing to you. You're the same woman who passed me over for a dancer who was less deserving."

Meredith's brow leaps at the word. "Deserving? I guess it all depends on how you define deserving."

This statement alone helps Della decode Meredith, the woman three times her age, her back-length hair grown long and grey in her privilege. Meredith views society from its apex, through the squint of blue eyes, at a world ranked and filed beneath her in an intricate taxonomy *according to* privilege, rather than more substantive things like character, competence, and ability. Regardless of Della having principal dancer talent and technique, there's a ceiling for a young, black woman with kinky hair from the dust bucket of Lumberton, North Carolina, and in Meredith's mind, Della has reached it. It dawns on Della that she's a victim of Meredith's discrimination as much she is a victim of her husband's sexual assault. Della erupts with every word she's held back since becoming a professional dancer. "You wanna know something, Meredith? That's precisely why, I've never seen anyone who looks like me – in any type of sought-after position – be as ineffective or aloof as you are. Because if *we* got the position, we had to be excellent to get it. We work twice as hard and have to be twice as good and finally be promoted years late. So, how do you think I feel, looking around at my peers, while knowing that there's a class of underprivileged ballerinas on Martin Luther King Avenue that would put these white dancers to shame if they had a fair shot. And yet the ones like me, who *do* make it through, are expected to be grateful just to be your tokens?!"

Meredith's glare is ripe with righteousness. "This is ballet not basketball, some sport we invented in America. The error in your thinking... tells you that because you're talented and can leap like reindeer, that you get to be at the center." Meredith clamps her mouth shut, fearing the escape of another canary.

"No, keep going," Della eggs on. "Sounds just fine in the mirror doesn't it? Not so much, when there's someone else in the room."

Meredith makes praying hands that rotate forward, "Let me explain it to you this way. You see, ballet started with the festivities to the royal wedding between lady Catherine de Médicis and Henry II of France…"

Della considers correcting Meredith, that ballet was already Italian Renaissance entertainment prior to that royal wedding, but Della decides not to disrupt Meredith's soliloquy because the woman's P.C. filter is failing her; therefore, Della anticipates being made privy to something that's never explained to ballerinas of color: what *they* really think about ballerinas of color.

"That wedding took place centuries before America was ever a notion – when the only thing thought to be that far out in the Atlantic, was the edge of a flat earth. There's centuries of tradition – European tradition, to uphold. So, you're not convincing anyone of anything with your aggressive turns, and vaults. It's as if you're flaunting – in our faces – the fact that you should've been principal all along." She sips her tea. "I don't like it. It looks militant."

"Did you just admit that I should've been promoted?" Della is now sure that Meredith's tea is spiked.

Meredith sets her cup in the saucer and says, "You're still so idealistic, Della, because you're still so young. You'll learn, as you mature, that life just works a certain way. I know how hard you work, thinking you'll become the *second* black ballerina ever to lead a major dance company. And I'd hate for you to one day come to the realization that you've wasted your better years on a ballet industry that will never darken. You're dating a rich man, I hear. Focus on that." Meredith sips again and slowly sets the dish on the end table beside her. "In fact, I wish you all would quit trying to shame us into including you, then once we let you in, all you do is complain about who we promote, or which dancers we bring to the stage. Try making your own stage—"

"—Great idea Meredith." Della jabs a pointed finger as if to pop Meredith's bubble. "Such a great idea, in fact, that you're gonna wire me one hundred thousand dollars, which I will then *use* to create my own stage!"

"Ridiculous." Meredith's head shakes three silent passes before laughter cranks at the back of her throat.

Della looks Meredith over – Meredith, the woman Della once thought of as caring and motherly. Wryly, Della comments, "I used to think you were too good for Yule. I'm glad to finally meet the real you." Della stands, turns, then marches on.

Meredith, still in mirth, calls, "Where're you going?"

Della, without a head-turn towards the question, replies, "I was assaulted! I'm going straight to the police!"

"*Wait*," Meredith yells, with an outstretched hand.

Della stops and turns with a ballerina's grace and a snide grin upon her lips. "Come again?"

Meredith hurries toward Della. "Come back. Sit. I'll wire you the money."

Della strolls back, saying, "I had much a smaller figure in mind, you know. I only wanted fair compensation for the years I was underpaid, and a pay raise going forward."

Meredith pays Della no mind, now strictly transactional, as she kindly asks for Della's account information.

As Della writes down the numbers, she says, "I was worried about the girls being subjected to Yule. But I shouldn't be subjected to you. You will receive my letter of resignation in forty-eight hours." Della hands the information over and says, "Go find you another token."

"Won't be hard at all," Meredith says, without even glance from her laptop screen.

Della notices, above the furnace, a pair of authentic African masks, like the ones located in the nearby Louvre Museum, which is filled with billions of dollars-worth of artifacts that Yule's countrymen had robbed from Africa; it inspires her to up the ante. "Make it hundred and fifty thousand, since you thought it was so funny."

Consequently, few words are exchanged. They verify the incoming wire. Wasting no time, Della is then escorted to the front door without a word, until a bitter Meredith comments, "Watch you end up blowing the money on shopping and vacations… You people's problem is not us. It's yourselves."

Della smarts, "Two, three years from now, your old ass *better* not come asking me for a job." The door is slammed at Della's back, as she hits long floral driveway to a sunbaked side street. She heads in the direction of the Eiffel Tower jutting above the Paris skyline.

Della had arrived at Meredith's doorstep, expecting to eventually spend half her savings for the flight home, but now she's leaving with more money than she'd ever had sitting in her account at once. She can buy a shuttle to the Charles de Gaulle International Airport and the flight home without a dent to her bank account, but for now she just walks as she takes in everything she's been through this incredible few weeks.

There's only one text from Miles, asking her whereabouts. The heartbreak hasn't lifted, but it isn't as heavy as it was initially. She had fallen to pieces when Pop confirmed that Miles cosigned the idea of her seducing Yule, which led to the assault. If Miles would risk her safety, he couldn't be a husband or even boyfriend of hers.

Della keeps on walking, seemingly drifting along the streets of Paris, a backpacker in leggings, dragging a large briefcase by the handle. She recalls how she'd placed the engagement ring in the drawer and left the chateau with a bleeding heart, but now Della walks with new life, new energy, new skin. She's invigorated by a pending reality that she never even had the audacity to dream – to form her own dance company, that will take in as many black ballerinas as it can hold, and give them the privilege of being at the center, the dignity of being sought-after, and the reciprocity of being rewarded and promoted on the basis of their dedication and talent.

Della walks a city street littered with signs and storefront marquees she cannot read. She passes by conversations she cannot understand. She focuses on the sound of her feet tramping and the rolling briefcase, not knowing if she's going in the right direction, but walking nonetheless, in the direction of the Eiffel Tower while wearing a smile that won't go away. She doesn't realize that she'd been walking for nearly a half an hour without a thought about Miles, because her head is now filled with visions of being on stage with a troupe of ballerinas without feeling like some sort of stain, without feeling like she's tolerated; she will be in rank with her sisters.

This feeling is surreal; it is indescribable and yet surprisingly uncomplicated. This feeling is as satisfying as it is large and vague and intimate. This feeling… is like falling in love.

Two Years Later...

Della is dressed in all white, crowned with a headdress and veil. An orchestra that she herself has commissioned, plays a score that is gentle, yet suspenseful.

Slowly, determinedly, Della walks. Her lead leg steps through the split of her gown; her instep arched, her pointed toe never leaving the floor, as if gliding. The heel torques inward to plant for the next dramatic step towards the waiting groom. She smiles lovingly, yet her eyes burn with the ambition to change the course of history for both Egypt and Rome. She is Cleopatra to be wed in hopes to protect her crown. Della, likewise, hopes this performance solidifies her footing in the upper-crust of performing arts.

Jabari, one of Della's top dancers plays Antony, but a different Antony than the reckless playboy that ballet usually portrays. He's a more Shakespearean take on the character, a more pragmatic Antony, with furry eyebrows and a stern gait.

Behind them, in the same technique that Della glides toward her groom, a troupe of gorgeous black ballerinas ease out of stage smoke, which curls through gleaming shafts of stage light. Della is sure that the reviews will skewer her for the set and wardrobe because the presentation leans away from European convention, despite leaning towards historical accuracy.

The tempo quickens. Dancers turn fleet of foot, their tiny steps, like little propellers skimming them across the stage like flying fish over the surface of water. By the climax of the heart-pounding score, the banners are out, splashing their color in the air like dragon fire, as dancers leap with the orchestra's resounding clash of brass cymbals. A pair of dancers stand apart and pull a banner tight. Jabari twirls into it, face first, his mold pressed in fabric, his silhouette, a flailing soul in the impermeable force at the crux of Antony's downfall; lust.

Della, meanwhile, focuses on her mark while trying not to focus on all the empty seats. Long gone is their inaugural season, when it was popular to embrace the new black dance studio who came out of nowhere to grace big venues like the Lincoln Center, Broadway, and the Pennsylvania Ballet Theatre.

Now in their sophomore season, ticket sales is down and influential columnists who once hailed them as ballet's Cinderella story, now harden their white gaze, approaching insult as much as professionalism will allow, how they dress lovely adjectives with ugly prefixes: dis-affecting, im-perfect, anti-climactic. Della has even endured sabotage from larger dance companies who'd underhandedly recruited her top ballerina.

The chip on Della's shoulder is now a boulder. She doesn't care that she'll catch editorial flak for reducing Cleopatra's eye shadow and ornaments to de-emphasize this "eastern" exoticism – the supposed lure to Antony's downfall – versus a supposed superior "western" values as the catalyst of Octavian's victory in war. This is what Meredith meant about taking what's *theirs* and turning it into whatever *we* want it to be. If cleansing racist tropes threatens them, then being their public enemy number one is Della's award of achievement. She has never felt more intersectional with a role than Cleopatra, who is the epitome of what Della has become: unapologetic.

The ballerinas on stage behind her, is all that matters. Della will fight for them at all costs, down to the pronunciation of their names, like the time she interrupted a member of the National Council for the Arts, *it's Kah-mee-sha* – her best friend who often gives flashes of soloist potential, now arriving at Della's side, cueing Della's series of fouetté turns.

The ballerinas who'd emerged from smoke (symbolizing Cleopatra's many contradictions) leap around her, creating the illusion where the whip of Della's working leg seems to churn them along like a turnstile, building speed. Della transitions into a series of turning leaps across the stage, followed by dancers leaping around her like a tornado growing with debris and hurling across the plains. Antony and Cleopatra, despite the insurmountable turmoil depicted here, was embroiled in a love affair so powerful that it robbed them of the agency to choose to be apart and uncomplicate their lives; they couldn't entertain the mere premise of a future without each other.

One of the greatest romances in the history of the world also happened to be a relationship of convenience; Antony needing Cleopatra for access to Egypt's resources, and Cleopatra needing Antony to restore Egypt's original borders. Della, deep in character, with the worry of these international concerns across her brow, looks out over the audience, and happens to recognize a familiar face.

It's Miles... Minus the dreads... Plus a woman.

Della's heart detonates while balanced en pointe, on one foot, the back leg fully extended parallel to the floor, and an arm stretched forward as if picking a low-hanging fig. Because of Miles, Della feels a sensation that's been trained out of her since childhood: dizziness.

She must concentrate twice as hard to survive the set without incident. Miles's lady looks very well taken care of, with her flawless skin, full hair, and a dress fit for a duchess. Della doesn't see Miles kiss or coddle his date, but at the same token, Della isn't able to get a long look at the pair until the scene of Cleopatra's suicide, where Della clutches a venomous snake to her breast. Spying through an open-eyed death, Della finally spots the thing that makes Cleopatra's death her own: the woman beside Miles wears a wedding ring.

Chapter 27
A Laughing Universe

Two years ago, when Della's solo international flight touched down in the states, her phone started going off with a slew of messages that Miles sent during the span of the ten-hour flight. Once Della was home and settled, she called. Miles apologized profusely. He had Pop come to the phone and admit that Miles had no knowledge of the plot that put Della in harm's way, and that the reason Miles didn't answer his phone was not out of guilt, but because he was down in the catacombs with no signal. Still, Miles asked for her forgiveness, which Della granted, but maintained that it's best to stay apart.

Miles, though blameless, was, by association, linked to the assault that Della was trying to forget in order to reclaim her inner peace. Even his voice over the phone made the trauma of Yule's attack swim to the surface.

When Miles came to retrieve his G-Wagon, he was embittered because he was denied a second chance. Months later, after a successful opening night for Della's Brooklyn Dance Studio, she drunk-dialed Miles and learned that her number was blocked.

Seeing Miles in the audience with a wife, Della now knows the reason she was blocked; his focus must've been on *her*. So soon? Maybe he proposed to this woman after only knowing *her* for a few weeks. And Della was foolish enough to think that what she and Miles had was special.

BEFORE showering or even shedding her costume, Della bolts, as if shot out of the dressing area. She heads toward the lobby to try to find Miles – if at all possible, in the audience's mass exodus. In Della's wake, there's a trail of turned heads, awestruck for realizing it was Cleopatra skirting by, then disappointed that there's now too many bodies between them to chase her down for a selfie.

Della experiences a mother's panic, as if a kid has vanished from her side. And with every moment lost, is the likelihood of recovering him in one peace – if only to shake into a thousand pieces. The nerve of Miles, she thinks. Coming here, flaunting his wife in her face.

Della wades in the bee swarm of people moving toward the exits. The only thing working in her favor is that very few of the bees are black. Outside the thick glass door, is a man Miles's height. Della takes off. She catches up to him halfway down twenty feet of concrete cathedral steps. The man who checks over his shoulder to see who has touched his arm, has the face of a melted mask. Della shrinks away, hoping her disappointment isn't mistaken as a reaction to his looks, "Thought you were someone else."

In a British accent, and the bellow of a nasally giant, he asks, "Mind a picture with my daugh-er?" The girl is a stairstep ahead of him, looking back in astonishment.

Della, though pressed to find Miles, cannot deny the starlit eyes of a child. "Of course," says Della.

While posing for pictures, the little brown-faced, aspiring ballerina reminds Della why she has sacrificed her personal life for the tireless work of running a dance studio, establishing a guild to facilitate affordable group insurance rates, and now getting a *second* dance studio off the ground.

Della, with her compass now restored, her first thought is, *What was I thinking? March up to Miles and say what? Expect what in return?* She wonders if it was really about Miles at all, or if she wanted his wife to witness how Miles reacts to her, and somehow feel like she is merely who Miles had settled for.

The father and daughter leave Della standing there shaking her head, thinking how silly she's being. Even the public square below looks as if it's the universe laughing at her, with a scene that's as random as a hot car dream. There's a street mime slowly tipping his hat. Just a few yards away, an upset pigeon boasts its chest to a stray black cat, it's back arched in fright. There's a protestor in the square, with a posterboard strapped over his body. In the distance, a pair of Clydesdales pull a tour wagon. Della is certain that the universe is speaking to her through the individual by the bird bath, posing for a picture: a fat lady with tiny hands who can't stop laughing. To beat all, there's Cleopatra standing knock-kneed on the steps of a salt white cathedral.

Della turns to go, and the impact of what she sees next steals her breath and bristles her neck hair.

Miles arrives at the top of the steps just in time to see Della turn toward the theatre, with that straight hair, black and shiny like a vinyl album whose grooves shake loose to strands, sling around in a cascading arc.

Miles starts coming down the steps and Della, instinctively, comes to him. They embrace. Miles explains, "I was waiting in the empty theatre… thought you might find me there." Della weeps on his chest, so Miles saves the explanations and holds her tighter, longer. "It's alright, baby. It's alright."

Della wonders if she's gone too far, embracing Miles like a long, lost love. Would his wife allow her at least this? Miles's hands slip inside the curtains of her wig, a thumb gently parting her lips. Della's teary eyes asks, *Are you sure?* He answers with a touch of lips so tender, yet loaded, that Della feels time itself grind to a halt, the random scene behind her surely frozen in an eccentric menagerie – clouds above, stock-still like gossamer glued against the blue sky; four wide oceans, for all Della knows, could be solid as quartz, yet Della's tears keep rolling down her face. The twenty-three-month-wide cavern in her heart pools with this moment. Miles tries to come away from the kiss, perhaps something he wants to say, but Della surges upward on the tips of her pointe shoes, calves flexed, head reared up, as she recaptures their kiss. Della's lips smears across his, swerving in the motion of no, and this is how she finally aborts the kiss, turning too far one direction, looking away, then down. "I was supposed to curse you out," she says.

Miles wears a dim frown, which cracks a smile like daybreak. "What?"

"Who is she?"

Miles looks back and around.

"Stealing a moment with me while she waits in the limo?"

Miles blinks with heavy eyelids. "Right. You never met Corine."

"Corine?"

"My sister, Corine. She's visiting from Bermuda."

The air that had filled Della's lungs in suspense, now empties in relief, leaving her panting, her eyes crazed. "Your sister!" Her hands sandwich Miles's face and she kisses him again, but quickly unplugs. "Wait… So, you're not married, but are you–"

"–No. I'm single. And I blame *you* for that."

"Oh really?" Della cranes back, waiting for the bullshit.

Miles gives her the handkerchief from his suit pocket with these words: "Because, I just can't have that what-if out there. I can't go on, thinking that maybe the biggest mistake of my life was fumbling our relationship."

Della nearly kisses him again, but she gets to thinking of all the changes she's been through these past two years. "I'm not the same Della you remember."

Miles points, in recognition. "Overthinking shit, like you're doing, right now? It's you, alright."

Della dabs an eye with the hanky, repeating, "I'm not."

"How," Miles challenges.

Della gains her composure, takes a deep breath, and tosses her hair back. "I'm a boss," she says. Her enthusiasm dampened by the recent cry, Della adds, "I've been a millionaire for seven and a half weeks now, bro – don't play wimmee."

"Ohhhh!" Miles shuffles back in celebration, a fist to his mouth. "That's what's up."

Della struts it out for all of two seconds, then swats it away, her cheeks packed with grins. It's all fun and games now, but Della honestly thinks it's an issue. When they first met, she was busy enough already, as a hyper-focused dancer, but now add to that, fulltime entrepreneur; a CEO herself? Della is pulled in too many directions by obligation to be a billionaire's wife, who's expected to always be at her husband's beck and call, like Sage had done for years. This is the elephant in the room, an elephant that follows Della and Miles into the building, sashaying its massive rump past the box office and then lumbering into the empty theatre to a waiting Corine.

Their conversation echoes in the big empty theatre. All the while, Della is hugged to Miles's body as if they're suddenly in a full-fledged relationship – just like that? After two years of nothing, an emotional kiss on cathedral steps and viola? Mile's arm is heavy around her shoulder, while he's promising his Disney-princess-looking sister that he and Della will visit her in Bermuda real soon. Della suddenly has this existential moment in the auburn carpeted theatre, looking an elephant dead in the face, the wrinkles around its eyes, deep as tire tread.

Miles had vowed to fly them over eight U.S. states, a peninsula, two seas, four islands and a strait, without checking with Della, so Della checks him. "Pink sand beaches, you say? Oh my! It's just that I'm so busy these days." She looks over at Miles. "I'd have to consult my schedule."

The way Corine quiets herself, and Miles's face goes dead, as if he's drained of mana, tells Della that maybe her execution was off; her entry into the discussion a bit forced, and the *oh my*, a bit facetious. The main instigator now lumbers away; the pachyderm, done with her, as well.

Miles responds, "Everybody's got a schedule to consult, Della. That goes without say."

Della, even in doubt of her execution, turns defensive. "Well if it goes without say, why is it so shocking to hear?"

Miles says, "Let me tell you something, Della."

"Please do," Della says, so sprite with interest, it's obviously a laid trap.

"I run a megacorporation. We know this, a'ight? And Corine here, is a consulate for the uh," Miles looks at Corine for help. "... on the counsel of Caribbean foreign trade... international. No?"

Corine chuckles, now Della's ally. An eyerolling Della comments, "*Please* help your brother."

Corine replies, "I'm actually laughing at both of you. Even in an argument you two are adorable."

Della explains to Corine, but for Miles to hear, "I have so much going on nowadays. I don't know that it's fair to him." She looks at Miles and realizes that she's a target in his sights, to which Della insists, "I have dreams, Miles."

Miles fires back, "Dafuck you suggest we do, *not* try?"

This new paradigm silences Della, as any potential clapback would seem to fight against the love she wants to fight for, but since Della must have the last word, she says, "I hate you."

"I know," he smiles, and before she knows it, Miles pulls her hand and she rolls into him like a dance. They're embraced again, kissing and giggling, Della pretending to escape his affection. Miles's kisses roam down to her neck.

"Oh no, don't do that," Della sings, in such a way that it means the opposite.

Corine clears her throat to signal that they're not alone.

Miles raises up, biting his lip with thoughts of what he'd do to Della.

Della backs away. "I better go change."

Miles, however, says he has to leave, head-pointing at Corine as the reason. It would be improper not to entertain his visiting sister and her family. He promises to call.

Della goes backstage to get dressed, but the dressing room, by now, is nearly empty, so she decides she'll change at home.

When she walks out through the theatre to take the front exit, she sets her bag down and zips it open. The Cleopatra wig and headdress has been on for so long she forgot it was there. The moment she reaches up to remove it, she hears someone call out, "Did you get my text?" Miles is still in the theatre, the bottoms of his shoes crossed and propped up on the back of the seat in front of him. "I had to send Corine on, man," he says. "I miss you," echoes in this large, empty theatre as if indicative of how immensely he misses her.

She'd already settled for takeout and immersing herself in work to avoid touching herself to thoughts of him, but now Della sighs and trembles with the images of this sudden change of plans.

"Mind if I join you," says Della. She comes over and sits next to Miles, and they have a conversation covering their time apart, surviving off of the memory of their short, but passionate time together, then Della asks, "Where do we go from here?"

Miles shows a stiff hand. "We just go, a'ight? If we talk about it, we become bound to our words."

"Don't we need clarity?"

"We go as fast as love will allow. I'd rather us get ahead of ourselves than behind."

Della's wig flares with her head turn. "No expectations? No dreams?"

"I do have a dream. I'm in it, right here with you."

Della looks at him fondly. "You're sweeter now." Her fingernail taps the chair arm, as she says, "I doubt you would've said something like that, the first go-round. Maybe it comes with age, Mr. Thirty," Cleopatra nudges. "With me, though, I have a vision, a very clear one. I remember you telling me how you and Pop were manufacturing black privilege in engineering. I wanna do the same for ballet. If things work out between you and me, I see us together as a power couple, fighting the good fight, creating opportunities. To do that, I'll need to build a school of ballet."

Miles leans forward and looks over at Cleopatra. "Are you negotiating the terms with me, right now? I notice that your vision doesn't mention children."

Cleopatra pulls her curtain of hair aside. "How many?"

"Six."

"I'll meet you half way. Three."

"Four, or no deal."

Della takes a deep breath. "Four, but under one condition: after the fourth child, the prenup becomes null and void."

"You really are a business woman, now." Miles says, with a smile. He extends a hand, "Shake on it?"

Della shakes his hand but says, "I want it in writing."

"Cool," Miles says. He uses the handshake to pull her in for a kiss, after which he comes away with a revelation. "This is probably my most romantic moment ever. You see, mom and Pop went into it with only their assumptions. Momma never got what she wanted and it made her bitter. You ought to see them now. Mom is finally getting the things she wanted and she don't even have an attitude no more. It's like they're young and in love again. Now that you and I have put it all out there, I feel like that's where we're headed."

They kiss again. Della holds his face there and says, "One thing, Miles. Can I trust you?"

Miles licks his lips. "I've lived under Pop's mistakes. I see the damage it can do, so I'm not about to repeat them. Besides, you're the last woman I've been with, and the way I see it, that will always be the case."

Della's eyes stretch wide in amazement. "You mean to tell me, that in two years you haven't… *I* haven't either." Her head shakes. "When I get you home tonight…" Words won't explain, so she doesn't try.

A moment passes in silence. Della removes her headdress, and says, "Did you hear about Yule?"

Miles huffs. "Yeah, that's fucked up." He'd died of a heart attack while having sex with a dancer.

Della adds, "The dancer he was in bed with, was my replacement."

"Aw damn," says Miles. He then asks, "What all you got going on tomorrow – well, never mind."

"What is it," asks Della.

"I'm flying out to Illinois tomorrow… thought it would be nice for you to see the family, but come to think of it, you probably don't wanna be in the same room as Pop."

"Got that right. Besides, I'll be conducting interviews tomorrow," says Della. She puts up a finger adding, "Oh, by the way, did I mention that I'm starting a second dance company? I jumped on the opportunity when one company folded because of tax problems. I booked all the venues they would've performed at – I'm talking premium venues. I'm even bringing on most of their dancers."

"Doing it big huh?"

"Yeah, but did you hear what I just said? I'm bringing on most of their dancers, white dancers."

Miles frowns. "I thought you was evening the odds."

"You see those empty seats tonight? The ticket sales have spoken. I'm trying to build a school. For that I need packed houses, which means, I can't do it on *our* talent alone. I need *their* dollars; therefore, I'll need to capitalize on their bias."

"Okay," Miles nods. "Now you're thinking like a billionaire."

"That might just be the best compliment you've ever given me." Della gets up, Miles tries to follow suit but Della pushes him back in the seat, and then straddles him. Gamely, he raises one eyebrow. It starts as a simple kiss, but passion takes over, for the hunger of two years behind them, and a fully imagined future before them, as sure as prophecy, it already feels like they are Mr. and Mrs. McKinnon.

Epilogue

After Yule's death, the Manhattan Dance Company had promptly relieved Meredith of her position. She has gone a year without work – a year in the sunken place, but she cleans up well for this sudden opportunity to become the artistic director of this unknown company. She comes into the interview looking the part of a polished disciplinarian, in a navy-blue skirt-suit, her grey hair up, in a modern geisha bun.

She glitches when she notices two black women at the conference table. She blanches when she notices that one of them is Della. Meredith looks to the whites, and asks, "What's she doing here?"

The head-turns domino to Della, but Kamisha speaks first. "She's the owner, you ole–" Kamisha stops because of a kick under the table from Della.

There's so much Della wants to say, but clears her throat in preparation to keep it professional. She says, "I think you and I know how this interview is gonna go."

Brazenly, Meredith says, "Oh, I bet I do. This is the only job opening within a five hundred miles, so if I do not get a fair interview, I'll be seeing you in court – just like you people do us. Let you see how it feels to be on the other side of things."

Della could tell by the unrest in the room that the 'you people' didn't sneak past anyone. Della realizes that maybe two years ago, Meredith's tea may not have spiked. Maybe her absent filter was early signs of mental decline. Della replies, "I'm not saying you won't get a fair interview."

Kamisha leans forward to look over at her friend. "After how she did you?"

Under the table, Della sinks her nails in Kamisha's leg to quiet her.

Meredith says, "Just so we're on the same page, when I say a fair interview, I mean hired. Because there isn't a resume in your pile comparable to mine. When your parents were probably in grade school, I was the principal dancer for one of the top companies in the states…" Meredith's outburst is rising to the level of spectacle, and her interviewers are now wowed spectators. "…When *you* were in diapers, I was the artistic director for the Paris Opera Ballet, the most prestigious dance company in the *world*. And ever since – until just recently – I have worked consistently with the top companies, including Manhattan Dance when I hired you."

Calmly, Della says, "Meredith, if you're suggesting that I hire you because you once hired me, that's bordering on nepotism."

Meredith grinds her teeth, some cynical retaliation brewing. "You can hide behind all the jargon you want, Della, but remember, I've got dirt on you."

Quite calmly, Della says, "If you have dirt on me, *do* tell, although I warn you, it may disqualify you as a candidate and discredit any litigation you may attempt."

Meredith's face sours. "Aw, you ole bastard you."

"Meredith, I'd say you've failed this interview before it even got started. I let it go, earlier, when you used the term 'you people,' and now you call me a bastard?" Della closes the folder and clasps her hands over it. "Your display of unprofessionalism here is not only intolerable, but I also feel threatened. Please see yourself out."

Meredith is already walking away, waving a dismissive hand, her words trailing off. "I know where you got the money to do all the things you're doing, and so God help me…" Della would've like to say, in turn, that she knows how 'your people' got the money and control over everything they gatekeep, but that would be improper.

Colleagues glance around in muted suspicion, but there would be no explanation, from Della, about this supposed dirt that Meredith has on her. Della turns her folders vertically and taps them level against the desk. "Well… that was our last scheduled interview for the day, so we can all take off early. See you guys tomorrow."

They get up and head out of the back office of the dance studio, walking across the empty practice floor, appearing to go their separate ways.

Della, though well within speaking range of Kamisha sends her a text. They head just down the street towards a bistro. Kamisha looks around and says, "Can you believe that ole hag?"

"You see right," says Della. "Girl, it took everything in me not to curse her behind out. The nerve of her," Della fumes. "She denied me the chance to make history, but got the gall to waltz into my office, acting entitled?!"

Kamisha's eyes thin. "Don't tell it to me. You had every opportunity to give it to Meredith, but you was sitting up there acting like a lil robot."

"I don't need to tell her what she already knows."

"Not for her, but for yourself. Get it off of your chest."

Della looks over at Kamisha, their mirror reflection in a storefront window walking alongside them. "Do they ever get it off *their* chest? Did Miss Belinda tell you why Callie was brought on after you, but promoted before you?"

"She tried to say Callie had more background in Romantic ballet versus classical, which is–"

"–Basically, a load of bullshit. I still haven't figured out what load of bullshit to tell the others about the artistic director position, since we're going with the applicant who has never worked at the professional level."

Kamisha says, "Maybe you can find some area she's particularly good at, and try to tie that into what we're trying to do as a company."

"As talented as she is," says Della. "She's been kept out by them. Their bias is leaving great talent out there waiting to be given a chance and flourish. You ought to see what she did at the Teen Studio of the year competition. She had those girls on point, ya hear me? Their technique, the synchronization, the way they maximized the space on the stage…" Della stares ahead, marveling at it all over again.

Kamisha says, "They'll only see that she's underqualified and black. They're gonna feel like you're reaching in order to give her the shot."

Della brushes a bang from over an eye and says, "They'll also see what she's capable of once given a shot. And that *is* the goal, isn't it?"

About The Author

Son of a carpenter and a nanny, Rod Palmer was born in a historic Gullah Geechie community in Charleston, SC. He received his degrees in creative writing and Afro studies at the University of South Carolina before becoming an author, and growing a list of eight published novels and counting. Currently he resides in Europe where he is a dedicated husband and girl-dad, enjoys travel and writing the next novel.

His other works are:

A Pimp In The Pulpit
The Work-Husband Caper
The Harvest
Karma Wears Versace
KWV II: Man Eater
The Waymaker
The Things We Bring To The Table